LONE SURVIVOR

LONE SURVIVOR

·

V. S. Meszaros

AVALON BOOKS
NEW YORK

Mes

Published by Thomas Bouregy & Co., Inc.
160 Madison Avenue, New York, NY 10016

Library of Congress Cataloging-in-Publication Data

Meszaros, V. S.
    Lone survivor / V. S. Meszaros.
        p.   cm.
    ISBN 978-0-8034-9870-9 (acid-free paper)
    I. Title.
    PS3613.E7886L66   2007
    813'.6—dc22   2007025078

PRINTED IN THE UNITED STATES OF AMERICA
ON ACID-FREE PAPER
BY HADDON CRAFTSMEN, BLOOMSBURG, PENNSYLVANIA

Chapter One

Rusty McBride rode into the settlement, a lean, tough young man leading a string of packhorses. Behind him for a good twenty miles lay the Shawnee Nation, and in front of him his destination, Fort Pitt. Right now he wasn't thinking of Fort Pitt. Instead, his piercing green eyes narrowed at the recognition of trouble.

A black-haired man was leaning negligently against an old building. His dark eyes, Rusty noted coolly, had been trained on the trader ever since he topped the ridge above the settlement.

Instinctively, McBride knew he was not a resident. He certainly didn't look like a farmer—not in an expensive shirt and boots. Nor did he look like a business owner. Fact was, he didn't look like a man who labored hard for his living. He looked like hundreds of other scroungers he'd seen hanging about places like this: men who didn't work and didn't intend to. To them it was smarter and easier just to take advantage of others. But just because they were plentiful, McBride didn't underestimate them. Hangers-on like this were dangerous. They saw every new person as a prospective victim. A man had to be vigilant out here or he'd find both his goods and his life taken. He had been knocking about the country long enough to have learned that right away.

A smile twisted Rusty's well-cut lips. He knew it wasn't him so much as his goods that were attracting this unwanted attention. He could almost feel those dark eyes drilling into his packs as if estimating their contents.

"Easy boy." He patted the horse's neck as it fretted a little, his rider's tenseness seeming to communicate itself to him. "Nothing to worry about. It's not a snake, but pretty close to it. Nothing I can't handle."

Rusty's discerning eyes seemed to skim only lightly over the black-haired man, but those eyes had noted him, taken stock of him, and classified him all in one glance. Trouble and then some—the words came forcibly to his mind. The man was displaying too much curiosity. Rusty minded his own business and he expected others to mind theirs.

Just as he came abreast of him, the black-haired man suddenly pushed away from the wall and stepped onto the dilapidated walkway.

"Hellooo, sir!" A grin dangled from his wide lips as he lifted his hat in mock respect to the mud-spattered trader. "What's your name?"

Rusty shot him a cold look, refusing to reply. He did not appreciate attention being drawn to him even if it was only from a few men playing cards who glanced up at the greetings, momentarily distracted.

"What you got in those packs? Eh? Surely do look heavy!"

Rusty's mouth hardened. The black-haired man saw it and chuckled. He knew he was irritating Rusty. That appeared to be his aim. As the horses went slowly by, the man hopped down onto the street and started to follow.

"Why don't you answer me? You sure aren't very friendly, are you, mister? I wonder why? Come down Salt Creek, didn't you?" the man speculated aloud, tauntingly.

That jolted Rusty. His head snapped sideways and his eyes turned to chunks of ice. The man was no longer just irritating. The mention of Salt Creek hit a raw nerve. His hand tightened on the reins. Now, how did he know about Salt Creek—unless he'd been there at the same time?

It had been miles back—in the afternoon—when Rusty became aware that someone was trailing him. He could sense it. The forest was familiar to him yet he had felt a difference creep in when he reached the creek. For one startled instant, a small sound had caused him to glance quickly over his shoulder, rifle ready. He had seen nobody, but out of the corner of his eye, a movement, as of someone diving for cover, had registered. Although Rusty had turned in his saddle and studied the area for some time, the movement did not reoccur.

So . . . he had not been mistaken. Someone had been there. Was that same man now walking right next to him and gloating over the fact that Rusty knew?

Cocksure that his words hit home, the man continued to saunter along. "Yes, sir. Nice day for a walk in the woods. Now, I wonder what you're carrying. Something valuable? Sure is dangerous hauling freight by yourself. You're alone, aren't you? Of course you are. Surprised you made it this far by yourself. Could be you're running out of luck!" His voice, glib and smooth, held a hint of a threat.

Seeing that Rusty still wasn't talking, the man swaggered over and stared at the big bags hanging over the side of each horse, getting so close Rusty's mount pulled nervously away. Rusty recognized such insolence that bordered on intimidation. The Indians used it on their enemies. They would stride right up to a man and stare him in the eyes, almost chest to chest, to see if he spooked easily. Rusty frowned, annoyed. He did not spook easily.

The black-haired man rubbed his chin in an openly reflective manner. "Hey, mister! I want to see what's in those packs! People around here got a right to know!"

Suddenly Rusty reined in and held himself still while his eyes honed in on the slick, calculating face.

His very stillness was a warning that the man did not recognize. Rusty allowed a chilly smile to flicker over his face.

"Go ahead and look," he invited. His voice when he finally spoke was soft, dangerous.

A light of victory sprang into the black eyes and the man leaned eagerly forward, hands reaching for the knotted cords. As soon as he came into range, his fingers touching the canvas, Rusty's foot kicked out, slamming into the man's face and sending him crashing to the ground.

"What do you think?" Rusty drawled. "Did you like what you saw? Want to buy some more? Come on closer." The rifle butt swung up in case his answer was in the affirmative.

The man scrambled up from the dirt, hand against his face while blood oozed through his fingers onto his shirt front. The black eyes flared hot and angry, yet there was also some satisfaction there that Rusty did not like.

"A man with as big a mouth as yours is, is bound to end up with a foot in it. Be glad I was wearing moccasins and not my boots!"

With that, Rusty picked up his pace and shot a menacing look over his shoulder. The man was standing in the middle of the road with a smirk on his face, but there was knowledge there too. Now he knew how far he could prod the trader before he reacted. It was knowledge the black-haired man would store away for later.

The horses didn't pause in their stride. Despite the man's presence, Rusty rode on into Bewilderness. He planned to stop here and had no intention of altering that for anyone. He was dead tired and so were his horses.

As he made his way down the poor excuse of a road, Rusty considered the man. There was a small possibility that the black-haired man had witnessed nothing and was merely guessing at the route Rusty had taken. He shrugged his broad shoulders. He didn't really care. The man was begging to be educated. Rusty didn't think someone as ignorant as that should be deprived of his schooling. Out here you have to draw the line so everyone knows where you stand. Rusty drew the line and the man crossed it. He got kicked. End of lesson.

There were still a few hours of daylight left. A cool breeze rustled down from the hills. It was refreshing now because the sun was hot on his back. When night fell, however, the wind would pick up and snap its cold edge through the settlement.

Sitting tall in the saddle, Rusty studied the loose scattering of buildings. Smoke curled up from the tavern's chimney and from the cook fires of a handful of cabins and half-faced camps. He had smelled it far down the trail.

It had been six months since he had come this way. To all outward appearances, Bewilderness looked just the same. The only thing different was the number of horses tied outside the tavern. There were a lot more than usual. Must be something going on here. Hopefully, it wouldn't concern him.

The tavern windows were ablaze with light and he could hear shouts and catcalls coming from inside. As Rusty neared, an old hound dog ambled across the rutted dirt road where he had been napping in the sun all day. Then he curled up in a corner on the tavern porch, ignoring the boisterous customers pushing through the doorway.

He led his packhorses down the road past some lean-tos and tents up to the Wilder place. At the stable door behind the tavern he stopped. He knew he could get food and lodging at Joe's.

Joe Wilder, the tavern owner and founder of the settlement, had named the place Bewilderness. Rusty had brought him here some years ago with a Delaware arrow deeply embedded in his side. When Joe awoke from a three-day fever, he looked around him and liked what he saw. This was not the land of milk and honey he had been searching for, but it looked good enough to him. Here he had stayed. Building a tavern, inn, and stables, he and his family had put down roots.

When Rusty reached the stable door, he opened it, urging his horses ahead of him. When he looked up, he was startled to see the black-haired man coming this way as well! His eyes were riveted on Rusty and his horses as he headed quickly for the door. *Oh no!* Rusty thought. *You're not coming in here!* Just as he led his last horse in, the black-haired man rushed up and reached for the handle. Rusty grasped the door and started to push it shut.

"Just a minute!" the arrogant voice ordered as if he was used to being obeyed. "I want to come in there! Stand aside!"

"Go somewhere else. This stable is full up!" The man tried to dodge in as the heavy door was closing. Rusty gave it an angry jerk. The man barely got his fingers out of the way before the door slammed shut. The bar fell down with such force, the door frame rattled. This time it was Rusty who smiled, though somewhat grimly. He knew in his heart that he wasn't finished with the matter.

"Brassy-faced bastard!" he swore out loud, not caring if the man could hear through the thick wood. He turned to his horses. They had traveled long and hard today and had earned their rest. He breathed in the familiar smell of hay, horses, and polished leather as he looked around.

It was a large stable. No need to stint out here where there was plenty of timber and enough land for the taking. On one side there were stalls for the horses. On the other were some bins, as well as piles of hay where a man could camp out if he didn't desire the company of others. Although usually not averse to socializing, on this trip he wished to avoid it.

He heard the sound of a door handle being tried. An unpleasant smile played across his face. If that bastard came in here, he'd tan his hide and hang it out to dry on a willow hoop! After a few yanks, the stranger apparently gave up for now.

Rusty dumped his gear in a corner and lifted the heavy sacks off his animals. Cool air filtered through the chinks in the walls as he stored his things in an unclaimed corner and removed the saddles. Afterwards, he led his animals to empty stalls and rubbed them down with care.

Just as he was beginning to relax, a small door began to open at the other end of the stable facing the tavern. Rusty whipped up his rifle.

"Open that door one inch more, you bold-faced son of a bitch, and you'll get a bullet right in your brisket!" he called in a cold voice. The door stopped moving.

"Lookee here, mister, this is my stables and I aim to come in!" an aggressive voice from the other side shouted back at him. Rusty lowered his gun and laughed.

"Come on in, Joe. Damned if you didn't scare the hell out of me!"

Joe grinned around the door and pulled it open all the way to greet the ex-ranger from Fort Pitt. Joe was a short, barrel-chested man with black hair plastered to his round head. His eyes crinkled when he saw the trader.

"Rusty McBride! Am I glad to see you in one piece!" The man hurried over and shook Rusty's hand in both of his. "We was worried fer ya. It's been a dangerous spring around here. Now summer's heatin' up with rumors of Indian trouble again—Miami, Delaware, you name it. I haven't seen you in a coon's age. I feared some hostile lifted yer hair!"

Rusty grinned. "No need to worry, Joe. I still have it. I've seen plenty of Indian sign around myself, though. Just last week I fished two bodies out of the Ohio and packed them over to Jezreel. They were both shot in the back and scalped."

"Murderin' savages!" Joe exclaimed. "A family up at Little Bushy Run was massacred a few weeks back. Three other families pulled up stakes and went back to Carolina. But as you see, there's always more comin' in to take their place. By the way, a wagon train pulled out a while back. You could catch up and travel with them if you've a mind to. Be safer that way, things bein' the way they are."

"Thanks Joe, but me and my horses need some rest."

"You need a room for the night, Rusty? I can shove someone out of a bed, if you don't mind sharin' a mattress with Lowell Carson."

"If it's all the same with you, I'll just sleep out here in the stable."

A spark of interest lit Joe's tired face and he glanced to where Rusty's gear was stored. He was quick to catch on. "Is that why you called me a son of a bitch?" His eyes twinkled.

"Sorry, Joe. Thought you were someone else."

"Plenty of them around. Someone followin' ya?"

"No, but I think I may have picked up a flea in town."

"Already? I thought you just got here?"

"I did, but I know trouble when it's glaring at me and my freight."

Joe nodded. "Always best to be safe. I'll send my boy Lonny over with some food. Just leave your dishes outside the door when you're done. Let you get some rest. You look all done in." Joe anxiously studied Rusty's handsome face. Weariness showed in his eyes, and his broad shoulders drooped with fatigue.

"I'm mighty beholding, Joe. And could I have some hot water too? I'd like to wash and shave." He produced a coin from his pouch.

"I ain't takin' no money from you, Rusty." Joe's face turned red. "You helped me out in the past when I needed it. You just tell my boy what you want." Joe rushed back to his boisterous customers. Through the open doorway, Rusty watched him disappear into the cooking area of the inn. Wilder was a good man. He was one of the few people Rusty had met in his life whom he could trust.

Through the open door, he could see the smoke-filled room where men gambled and drank, bragging loudly. With the freight Rusty carried, it wasn't a smart idea to mix with them just now. He had to stay sober. But then, he never was much of a drinking man.

As Lonny, a boy of about twelve, brought a heaping plate of food and a mug of coffee and placed them on a barrel top, a party of eleven riders came tearing down the road kicking up stones and clumps of earth as they thundered into Bewilderness. They came to a skidding halt in front of the tavern in a cloud of dust, horses rearing and pawing the air. The rowdy bunch looked hell-bent for trouble. As they dismounted, the youngest of the riders pushed his way ahead of the others aggressively. He was a skinny, raw-boned youth who elbowed through the crowded doorway. When the gang entered the tavern, the raucous noise was kicked up a few more notches.

"Who are they, Lonny?"

"There's a party of surveyors and packhorse drovers been sent by the Virginia governor. They're settin' out a settlement down south a here and they come by almost every night to drink. They're law-abidin' enough up 'til then. After a few drinks, all hell breaks loose. They pick fights with anyone and everyone. Especially that skinny one. He's a mean little cuss. Even pushes the peaceable citizens into fights just fer the fun of it."

The noise got louder. A strident voice made some crude comment that sent the giddy, uncouth rabble into loud guffaws. A shouting match followed. A pewter dish clattered against something hard, then they heard the rumble of tables being moved against the walls and out of the way. Things were heating up to an all-out brawl.

"Them louts!" Lonny complained. "Pa calls the leader the Bantam of Bewilderness. They come in drinkin' Black Dog Rum. Then they wash it down with a small keg of Pigeon Squeezin's Whiskey. That's Pa's own brew. And it ain't the pigeons he's squeezin' if ya get my meanin'? Pa says it'll grow hair where you ain't never had it before, whether you want it there or not. Even

Daniel Boone drops by to squeeze a few pigeons ever' now and then!"

Rusty smiled. He had heard about Joe Wilder's homemade brews. He had even tried one once—but only once.

"Lonny. I saw a man when I first came into town; tall, black-haired, and dark eyes. Handsome, but brazen and unpleasant."

"I know who ya mean," Lonny said immediately, as if there was a bad taste in his mouth. "I seen him. He's been around afore."

"Know anything about him?"

"Just that he's meaner than a wolf. Never gives ya the time o' day. Just keeps to hisself," Lonny said, taking up his tray. "Well, Rusty, I gotta go mop up after that bunch. I'll bring ya some hot water later so's you can clean up."

"I'd like that." Rusty rubbed his unshaved jaw ruefully. "Now that I'm back in civilization"—some more noise broke out just then—"or near to it. Oh, and Lonny, see what else you can learn about that man. Here." He tossed him a coin. "That's for any information you find out."

"You don't have to pay me, Rusty, Pa said—"

"This is extra work." He winked. The boy grinned and pocketed the money.

"Thanks, Rusty, I'll see what I can do." He went out whistling.

That was the problem with this country, Rusty mused. There were too many strangers—men who went from place to place where no one knew a thing about them. They could be here one day and then disappear into the forests for years. Some men liked it. They hated to be tied down to any one place or home. But for others—the dishonest and these who preyed on the helpless—it was merely an easy way to escape justice.

When the boy left, Rusty pulled over a couple of sacks of feed next to the barrel and dined in style. He hadn't had a home-cooked meal in quite a while and had been looking forward to it on the trail. He was beginning to feel relaxed and contented. After a while, even the din from across the way ceased to bother him.

After dinner, the young trader stood before a dimly lit piece of mirror and shaved off four days' growth of beard. He heard an uproar, then watched disinterestedly as a frontiersman came flying out of the tavern doorway to land in a heap in the road. The tipsy man struggled to his feet and staggered away, done with socializing for the night.

Back in the tavern, tables and chairs were scraped along the wooden floor back into place. The argument, apparently, was settled to everyone's satisfaction. Rusty could hear the surly troublemakers order a small keg of Black Dog Rum, then finally settle down to the serious business of drinking themselves into a stupor.

Clean and fed, Rusty lay down comfortably on his bedroll, then thought about the man who had confronted him. After reviewing the events of the day, he decided that this was the man whom he had glimpsed in the woods near town. But he hadn't been on his trail for long. Rusty would have noticed that. He was an ex-ranger, one of Captain Maxcy's best. He would know instinctively if he was being followed.

No, he had picked up this one just recently. Of course, the man would have noticed the unusually heavy load his horses carried. It was doubtful he had figured out it was silver Rusty was freighting into Fort Pitt—silver he had traded for with the Shawnee. Rusty had a bad feeling that the man wouldn't give up until he found that out. But if the stranger thought he could rob him of his silver, he was dead wrong.

Rusty had been on his own since he was fourteen. No stranger to work, he had been a farmer, a ranger, and a scout for the Army. He had years of struggle and hardship behind him, years during which he had built up his trading post. By dealing honestly he had gained people's respect, their trust, and their business. The Shawnee would part with their silver to no other trader but him. They knew he wouldn't cheat them like so many other white men had in the past.

He was not about to let some greedy no-account strip him of one of the richest shipments of his life. He'd get it to Fort Pitt all right, and no one was going to stop him. Rusty might look like an untried cub to that scrounger, but he was eight-and-twenty, deceptively strong, and a dead shot. If that man took him for an easy mark, he was in for the shock of his life.

Darn! Rusty had meant to rest the horses here for a few days. Now he was beginning to feel that if he got shed of Bewilderness, he'd be better off. And if that black-haired lout wanted to follow, why he could just pack away his fancy boots and come a running after him! He just might do that. Rusty knew that for this much silver, a man could be robbed, even killed . . .

In the tavern across the way, James Brisco sat down to have a meal. From a window he had been watching the activity around the stable when that trader came in with his freight. Apparently, he was a good friend of the innkeeper. Brisco heard the name Rusty McBride mentioned. The name meant nothing to him, but that freight of his did. It weighed on his mind plenty. Like a gnat, it bothered him.

No doubt about it! That yokel had been as nervous as a groom on his wedding night when he had surprised him in the woods today. Only one reason for that, and that was because he was packing something valuable.

He beckoned to Lonny who came over for his order. "Who's that trader sleeping in the stables? He looks familiar," Brisco lied.

Lonny shrugged. "Don't know nothin' about that."

"What's he carrying in his packs?"

"Is he carrying somethin'?" Lonny seemed surprised.

"How long is he staying?"

Lonny thought about this and decided, finally, that he didn't know that either.

Brisco gave up on the boy and ordered a meal.

The boy looked speculatively at Brisco. "Do ya think you can chaw on venison stew with your jaw all bloated?" Lonny wondered as Brisco touched his cheek gingerly.

Brisco got riled. "Just bring me some soup!"

Lonny turned away so Brisco didn't see him grin as he gave the order to his mother. Brisco wandered over to the bar to try to pump the elder Mr. Wilder but got nothing from him either.

"I don't know nothin' about nobody, mister," he growled at him bluntly, ending any further attempts at conversation. He asked a few more people, but they were more interested in eating than talking.

It didn't matter, Brisco figured as he sat down to eat. The Wilders' very lack of communication merely whetted his curiosity about the trader. Must be something they wanted to hide.

Brisco thought again about those packs. He didn't think they contained rifles, but McBride could be carrying goods just as valuable like salt or potash. Animal traps would bring in a lot of money too. Furs, cloth, trinkets—there was a serious shortage of everything on the frontier. A man could make himself a nice profit selling those goods at one of the forts.

Brisco could always wait it out until McBride left, then waylay him on the trail. But first he wanted to know what freight he carried. He'd like to take a look at it tonight, so he could calculate his profits in advance—see if it was worthwhile to stalk the man in the first place.

Of course, if McBride found that his packs had been tampered with, he'd know who it was. He might cause trouble, and he seemed to have a lot of friends around here. Pity, if he'd been a complete stranger he could kill him and rob him and no one would care. Everyone would just assume he had passed through. People with friends were harder to dispose of. No, he'd have to find a way to look in those packs without the trader knowing. That should be easy. He couldn't stay in the stable all of the time.

While these thoughts flittered pleasantly in his mind, he sat back and watched contemptuously as the rowdy customers plagued the pretty serving maid. They would call to her and try to catch at her skirts as she rushed past then with loaded trays. Deftly, she managed to slip away from their grabbing hands and scurry off to the safety of the cooking area as quickly as she could.

"Ring-tailed boors!" she cursed under her breath, setting the tray down with a crash. "I hate them!" Lonny and Joe Wilder could only nod in agreement.

Brisco felt no concern whatsoever for the girl's uncouth treatment. If you work around men like this, you take what you get. Brisco had no gentlemanly instincts. He did have a cool brain, however. Suddenly, he saw an opportunity here. He saw a way that he could get a look at the trader's freight with little risk to himself. He thought of the man sleeping in the stable then looked consideringly at these hotheads, drunk and raring to fight. The girl was the perfect ploy.

Leaning back in his chair, he listened to their loud-mouthed leader grumble into his rum about how unfriendly the girls in this settlement were. Now was Brisco's chance to start things rolling.

He scraped his chair closer to them and said in a voice tinged with insult, "Well, my friend, you don't seem to have much luck with the ladies."

"You speakin' to me, mister?" the leader snapped.

"Yes. She's a real good-looking girl. But I don't think you're her type." He looked around the group and gave a short derisive laugh. "Any of you!"

"I suppose you think you are!" the leader snarled, taking in Brisco's clean-cut good looks.

"Not me! I'm not pretty enough. She keeps her man hidden away in the stable to protect him from you rough-and-tumble men. He doesn't want to dirty his hands with you, so he even takes his meals out there. If I know women, she'll probably go out to meet him later!"

The men, scalded by his insults to their manhood, scowled in the direction of the stables. One of the more skeptical ones asked, "How do you know all this?"

"I saw him riding in. Tall, good-looking man. White teeth. The kind women like." He deliberately raked the leader's rather scrawny build and grinned. "When I asked him if he was from Virginia, he said, 'Hell no! I'm no hayseed! I'm a Pennsylvania man!' "

Another man slammed down his tankard, sloshing liquid in the air and into his own face. "That does it!" he yelled as ale ran down his face. "A real purty boy, you say? Maybe when we get through with him, he won't be so danged purty! After we clean up the floor with him, we'll send him back to Pennsylvania in a pine box!"

The leader yelled, "Ain't no better man than a Virginia man!" Everyone cheered. "Ain't no better lookin' neither! Let's go pay this man a visit. He might keep early hours. C'mon men!"

The men got up, scraping their chairs back hard and stomped out of the room in a group, affronted. They were on a mission. Staggering over to the stable door as quietly as they could, they rolled up the sleeves of their filthy homespun shirts all ready to do battle.

Lonny had heard most of the conversation as Brisco baited the men into an encounter. Then he ran to his father, shouting, "Pa! That no-good pack of souses is goin' fer Rusty!"

Joe was furious. It was a sad day when a friend of his couldn't have a decent rest in his own stable without being bothered. "They are, are they?" He picked up a four-foot length of lumber from a barrel of odds and ends used for keeping the peace. He heaved it reflectively.

"Pa, are ya sure you want to use the big board? You always use the medium-sized one."

"Uh-huh! This one's special for smashin' empty noggins!" He gave it a few powerful practice swipes through the air, then headed for the stable.

As the gang silently stumbled into the stable and made a ring around the dozing figure, Brisco moved behind them near the freight. Once they knocked the trader unconscious, he'd just see what McBride was carrying in those heavy packs.

As the intruders stared at the sleeping man, their leader got heated up all over again. By golly, he was a purty boy! He stared at the reddish-brown curling hair and straight nose. He probably had white teeth too! And he didn't snore! That made him even more angry. He strode up to him in a magnificent rage. He'd show him!

Rusty had just started to nod off. The noise next door receded to a dull roar and didn't bother him anymore. Bone tired from his trip so far, this was the first time in weeks he'd enjoy a decent sleep under a roof.

Slam! A blast of pain shot through Rusty's face as his head snapped sideways. His eyes flew open. Standing over him was a tall, thin young man, obviously drunk. His eyes were wild, hair in a frenzy as he tried to focus on Rusty's wavering face. He was clenching and unclenching his fists. Seeing that he had Rusty's attention now, he backed up and stood, legs apart, fists planted on his hips, his jaw stuck out aggressively.

"My name is Andy Jackson and I can beat up any man for a hundred miles around! Huh!" He nodded his head as if daring Rusty to disagree.

Rusty looked around him. The lantern light had dimmed and he found himself alone in the gloomy stable surrounded by eleven thugs ready to take their turn with him. They swayed unsteadily on their feet, but it didn't mean they weren't dangerous. Their leader, in particular, was out to draw blood.

Furious, Rusty jumped to his feet rubbing his jaw. It was the fury of someone awakened out of a sound sleep.

He took three running steps towards the drunken Jackson and slugged him in the eye with his right, then hooked him in the side of his head with his left. A final powerful slam to the stomach was enough to do him in. All of Rusty's anger at being awakened was in that last punch.

Jackson, already unsteady on his feet from too much drink, reeled backwards, falling hard against one of the stalls. He slid down on his back and landed with a hard smack on his rear end. He stared at Rusty as if he couldn't believe his strength or audacity.

Pushing on the ground with one hand, he tried to get up. As he rose on shaking legs, Rusty smashed him in the stomach twice. Jackson fell back against the partition again but did not fall. Rusty slammed his fists into Jackson's ribs and jaw until, unable to maintain his tenuous foothold on the floor, Jackson fell down.

The ring of shouting, jeering men grew silent. Outraged, one of them finally spoke up. "That there is Andy Jackson! You can't do that to him! No one can do that to him!"

Rusty slung around, a mean look on his face. "You want to come over here and say that to me?" he invited with cold eyes.

The man didn't. "You can hear me from there," he said, backing off. Rusty glared at the others watching, all in various stages of inebriation. Mouths agape, they stared at Jackson's still form in disbelief.

"Get up! Yer Andy Jackson, remember? Andy, don't ya remember nothin'?" Some of them urged him to get up and fight. "Ain't ya gonna teach that purty boy a lesson?" Jackson could only gasp, then his head lolled to one side.

"Now get that lush out of here or I'll do the same to the lot of you!" Startled at this direct attack on themselves when they had come to be mere spectators, they rushed over in a group to help their fallen comrade. Between the ten of them, they managed to get Jackson on his feet, then stumbled out of the stable with him almost erect. Jackson's left eye was purpling and swelling. By his groaning, his friends knew he would have a pretty collection of bruises tomorrow, particularly on his posterior, which already looked to be giving him great pain.

Rusty went to the door to make sure they left. Jackson's friends managed to get him only a few yards before losing their grip. Staggering a few steps, the man who would one day be president of this great land went tumbling into the horse trough.

"Get me the hell out of here!" a sputtering Jackson

demanded. His friends, too drunk to do anything more, could only collapse to the ground with the unaccustomed exertions.

"I want a drink," one mumbled. "Tavern keeper! Get me a drink! Ronny! Donny!" he called. The name finally came to him through the fumes in his head. "Lonny!" Immediately, everyone started calling for Lonny.

Rushing across the tavern yard armed with his plank, Joe Wilder called to his son, "If they want a drink, they can climb up the steps and get it! I ain't servin' no drinks in the road." Then he yelled to Jackson and his friends, "Get that drunk outta my horse trough. I don't want to have to refill it if he drowns in it!"

Shaking his head at the drunken bunch, Rusty turned back to his bed. He realized with a start that not everyone had left. His gaze settled on a solitary man standing within two feet of his gear. It was that black-haired bastard again! He could see the man's toe edging towards the canvas covering his freight! That obnoxious, persistent sneak was still trying to see into his packs!

"What the hell are you doing there!" Rusty barked. "Get away from those things before I throw you out!"

The handsome stranger smiled, but his foot continued to edge over. It started to lift one flap. Rusty's hand went to his rifle. He brought it up to his shoulder and aimed it at the man's face. "You heard me, mister. One more move towards my things, and you'll have a hole in the middle of your head."

It was said in a deadly voice that not even the likes of this bold-faced snake could mistake. Rusty's unflinching stare down the forty inches of rifle barrel went with it. There was no doubt but that he would shoot.

Joe and his son had come just in time to see the man and hear Rusty's threat. Joe was still clutching his stout stick. As it happened, he was too late to use it—or was he? Father and son watched silently, ready to jump into action if necessary.

The stranger's eyes flickered to where the innkeeper loomed threateningly in the doorway. No, this was not the time or the place for a showdown. He was a patient man. There would be time to have it out with the trader later.

He made himself shrug as if it was of no consequence. "Take it easy. I was just here to watch the fight," he lied. Rusty's eyes went to the toe of the boot as it still nudged the flap while he spoke. The sound of a rifle being cocked fell into the silence.

"Fight's over. Leave."

With a short, contemptuous laugh, Brisco turned on his heel and walked out of the stable. Rusty didn't lower his rifle until he heard his steps die out.

Joe came all the way into the stable. "You all right, Rusty?"

"Thanks. They just woke me up, that's all. They thought they were playing a practical pleasantry on me." Then he motioned to the door where the man had disappeared. "He's another matter. That gent was trying to go through my packs. I don't think he was with the others."

"He wasn't. Want me to slap him on the head with my board?" Joe asked hopefully. "Might improve his manners some."

Rusty's smile was stiff. "Not yet, but you might have to one of these days. He strikes me as a man who doesn't give up. Could you keep an eye on him? Maybe you could find out who he is?"

"I'll try to, though he's not well liked," Joe admitted. "You gonna be all right here alone?"

"Sure. And if anyone sneaks up on me at night, he'll find I'm a light sleeper and can't help shooting if I'm disturbed." They all laughed, then the two Wilders went back to the tavern.

Things were quiet back at the tavern. Brisco seated himself again and stared into the fire. He had to plan. That trader was mighty quick to pull that trigger. He must have something very valuable to make him so touchy. There must be a way to find out what it was.

In the meantime, Brisco thought to disappear for a while—maybe allay the trader's suspicions. He had heard McBride would be resting up for a few days before pulling out. If he kept out of sight for a time, he might relax his guard.

In the meantime, he decided to scout the trail up ahead for an ambush site. It was more than probable McBride's destination was Fort Pitt. It was the biggest of the forts in the area and the best market for his goods. Of course, Brisco wasn't going to take any unnecessary risks himself. His immediate problem was to find some men to help dispatch McBride into the next world as expeditiously as possible. Once he took to the trail, he could do what he pleased.

Chapter Two

Ben Allyn stopped and stared. He couldn't believe it. His canoes were gone! The two that he spent the last month painstakingly hollowing out with an ax weren't there. His young face hardened. Kenny Minks! No wonder he couldn't find him anyplace in the settlement. Instead of paying for the canoes like he promised, he'd just taken them.

Disillusionment turned to rage. That money was to have gotten him through the coming fall and winter. Now what was he going to do? He had only a little money. He had refused other jobs because he thought Minks would pay him well. Now he had nothing.

Ben ran up and down the riverbank searching for any sign of the canoes. He walked several miles before harsh reality set in, and he finally admitted to himself that Minks had probably stolen them hours ago. He may have even taken them last night when Ben had told him he was almost finished. Minks had timed the theft perfectly too. It had rained just enough to wash away any tracks Minks would have made. Ben would never find him now.

His fury tinged with hopelessness, Ben stomped on to the settlement. Heading for the tavern, he noticed offhandedly the usual drunken crowd there. Most of them were sprawled on the ground around the water trough. He didn't waste thought wondering about it, nor did he care. He was too hopping mad.

Then he caught a glimpse of one of the drunks climbing out of a horse trough. He was a thin, wiry man with his hair sticking up in shocks where he had tried to wipe it dry. Seeing the younger man coming towards him, and Ben Allyn looking a mere pup at twenty, he immediately jumped into his way.

Pushing up his sleeves preparatory to delivering a thrashing, Andy Jackson bellowed, "Hey you, boy! Lookee this way! My name is Andy Jackson, and I can beat up any man for a hundred miles around! Huh!"

The drunk was the last rotten straw in Ben's miserable day. Ben punched him in the eye, sending him flying back into the horse trough. Inside the trough Jackson groaned, clamping his hand to his other eye. Now both would be purple.

It was nearer to 10:30 when Ben entered the tavern and threw himself into a chair. The place was almost empty, now that the local riffraff had left. The serving girl and Lonny were cleaning off tables and righting chairs. Only one other customer remained.

Joe had seen Ben enter and noticed his angry face. "What's the matter, son?" he inquired sympathetically.

"That damned Kenny Minks!" he said, slamming his hand on the tabletop. It was a stupid thing to do. His hands were gashed and bruised from scraping out the canoes. "He took those canoes I was making for him and didn't pay me. Not a cent!"

Wilder knew what a hard-working, respectable young man Ben was. He might seem stiff sometimes, especially among women, but a better man couldn't be found in Bewilderness. Joe had always tried to steer work his way.

Joe was silent a moment, remembering how hard Ben had worked on the canoes. "You'll come on him again," Joe tried to comfort him. "He won't stay hidden long. Always into somethin'. You can git your money from him then." Then he added, "If he comes this way again, I'll collect it for ya." He nodded to his barrel full of timber pieces. "They're very persuasive."

"Thanks, but I'll get it from him, all right. I'll beat it out of him if I have to!"

"You watch him, Ben. He carries a knife under his arm. Don't let him see you a-comin'." Ben looked at Joe's concerned face and tried to smile. It was somewhat wobbly.

"I won't. Don't worry, I'll think of something," he said, although he didn't know what.

"What you need is a good meal." Mrs. Wilder had come up and listened compassionately to his story. Ben was such a nice, polite young man. "You just set over there in the corner, and I'll bring you something."

Ben turned red and shuffled his feet nervously. "I can't, ma'am. I–I don't have much money and I couldn't pay—"

"You hush now and set down. Pay me! I never heard the like. Can't a body do somethin' for another body without wantin' to be paid? You just set, and I'll bring you some nice meat and potatoes and some fresh baked bread."

Embarrassed, he thanked her and retired to the table she indicated. At the table across from him sat a dark, good-looking man. A stranger. Ben ignored him and sat down.

Mrs. Wilder returned with a huge plate of food, bread, and some cheese. "I'll just pack the rest of that away for you when you're finished." She smiled.

Ashamed at how low he'd sunk—he'd never been a grub-hustler before—he ate slowly as if afraid to enjoy it. Ben, however, was young, healthy, and hungry. Before he knew it the food disappeared. With a grateful smile he accepted the bread and cheese from Mrs. Wilder, who packed it for him and left it next to his chair. He was feeling better, but he was still infuriated with Kenny Minks.

As he nursed a cup of hot coffee between his hands, he finally took notice of the dark-haired man opposite him. To his surprise, he realized that the stranger had been listening carefully to his conversation with Joe. Ben didn't think he liked that. He looked at him.

The man nodded then got up and left the tavern. After that, Ben didn't give the stranger a second thought. Revenge was uppermost in his mind.

Not wanting to spend more time than he had to near Jackson and his worshippers, Ben stood up and said his good nights to the Wilders. Then he made his way back to his lonely camp.

Chapter Three

When Lonny came to pick up his breakfast dishes the next morning, Rusty questioned him about what had happened in the tavern to precipitate things.

"It was that dark-haired man started it all, Rusty. His name is James Brisco. I heard someone talkin' about him. Jackson and his men was takin' an interest in Lucy, our servin' girl, and she was ignoring them. They was gettin' heated up about it, ya see? And this Brisco feller started to egg 'em on. Sayin' that she wasn't interested in them on account of she had somethin' better tucked away in the stable waitin' for her—you! Sayin' you was hidin' there 'cause ya didn't want to be sociable with the likes of them. Bein' likkered up, they got plumb riled. He was nudgin' them into a fight and they was itchin' to visit you."

33

"I figured it was deliberate," Rusty said thoughtfully. "He sure picked the right men to keep me busy while he tried to look through my bags."

"Is that why he done it?" Lonny's young voice dripped with contempt. "He's a petty thief?"

Not so petty, Rusty thought to himself. If the boy only knew.

"Pa and me wondered why he was hangin' around here doin' no work. He's always in the inn of an evenin', but he don't drink much."

"Tell me, Lonny, does he associate with anyone?"

"Associate, is it? Ya mean, like friends? Nope. He'll sit down and make some talk, mostly with newcomers in town." Lonny lowered his voice. "Some of them people complained that their money was missin'." Lonny gave a sigh of regret. "But no one could say who done it, them bein' drunk and all."

"What about those surveyors? Did he come to town with them?"

"No. Brisco slinked into town all by hisself a few days after they come. 'Course now, he do like to go traipsin' about in the woods. There's a few men camping down by the shore. Some of them don't never show their faces in town. They come and go without no one knowin'."

"Probably wanted someplace, or up to no good," Rusty said grimly.

"Probably are," Lonny said cheerfully. "So it's best

they stay outta Bewilderness. Got enough problems keepin' the law-abidin' citizens in line."

"You handle the citizenry; I'll handle Brisco."

"You think he'll try to rob you after last night?" Lonny was surprised. He didn't think Brisco was that stupid.

Rusty got out his rifle and started to clean it. He recalled the impudence Brisco possessed to brazen it out even while he was weaponless and looking down the length of Rusty's rifle. "He'll try again. He's nervy, real nervy. Just the kind of man you can't turn your back on."

After Lonny left, Rusty did some thinking. He figured the sooner he left Bewilderness behind him, the better. Brisco was proving to be a thorn in his side. He was wishful to know what freight Rusty was packing and was not at all shy in going about it. Although he seemed alone in his curiosity, who knew if he had some hirelings waiting someplace nearby.

Would the man follow him once he left the settlement? Now, that depended on whether Brisco found out Rusty carried a load of silver. Right now he was just nosey, wondering if he could filch something saleable from him to buy some more frilly new shirts. Once the bastard found out all those packs were filled with prime silver, there would be no stopping him. He'd follow Rusty from here to the gates of hell to get his hands on that much money!

Damn his knowing eyes! He'd touched Rusty on the raw by messing with his packs and he knew it. Mild interest had turned to overwhelming curiosity. Yes, Rusty had been quick to hustle him out of the stable. Brisco was no fool. He'd realize the trader had something to hide. Well, there was nothing Rusty could do about it. It was inevitable that someone was bound to find out eventually. He was lucky to have gotten this far without meeting up with thieves. Now that he'd met one, he'd have to deal with him.

Rusty decided to make the first move. He didn't like it, but his hand was forced. The longer he stayed, the more time it would give Brisco to plan and prepare. Rusty was in no mood to give him the time. He did not like waiting to see what others did first. He'd play his own hand and let them play theirs.

The first thing he would do was ask about the settlement for more information about the man calling himself James Brisco. Next, he'd tell Joe to mouth it about that he was pulling out at the end of the week. Brisco had seen how tired the horses were. Maybe he'd buy it, maybe he wouldn't. If he did, he would believe he had time to work on Rusty. And that was what Rusty needed—time—if only for a good head start. Tonight, then, he could slip out of Bewilderness altogether. Let Brisco try to track him then! He had not been one of Maxcy's Rangers for nothing. He knew a few tricks that Brisco didn't.

Rusty went over to the stable door at a sound from

outside. He watched with mild interest as a rider galloped down the road that led out of the settlement. In a few minutes the horse and rider disappeared. It was Brisco. His bedroll and pack were tied up behind his saddle as if he was pulling up stakes and clearing out. Although he hadn't looked in Rusty's direction he certainly knew Rusty was watching. He wasn't exactly being quiet about it. He made no effort to hide his activity.

Rusty stood leaning against the doorjamb for a good half hour, waiting for him to reappear. He didn't, but the young trader wasn't fooled. He knew damned well Brisco wasn't leaving for good. He was too crafty to give up. Too crafty, too obvious, too confident. He motioned to Lonny when he saw him leave the tavern.

"Son, I'm going to look around a bit. See what I can find out. Can you watch my gear?"

"Sure thing. Looks like that Brisco feller took off outta here a while back like he weren't returning." Lonny inclined his head towards the trail Brisco had taken.

"Maybe that's how he wanted it to look." Rusty didn't sound very enthusiastic. "But you never know which way a snake will twist, Lonny. Somehow I just don't trust that man." He smiled at the boy. "I won't be gone long."

First thing, Rusty wandered over to the blacksmith's. "'Day, Ned," he greeted going into the smithy.

"'Lo there, Rusty." Ned had a brisk business and was busy shoeing horses. "Stables all right fer ya? You'd be more comfortable sleepin' at the inn. Just stuffed Wilder's mattresses with new corn shucking. Mighty nice to lie on. Smells good too."

"No, thanks." Rusty sat down on a huge tree stump. They said Ned Salem just cut the tree down and built his smithy around it. "I'd rather stay in the stable."

Ned sent him a shrewd look. "You mean you got to watch yer stuff, eh? Heard about yer run-in over to Joe's. I expected ya to come askin' about Brisco, him tryin' to get at yer freight and all." He saw Rusty's surprise and grinned. "Word travels fast around here. I got it from Lonny this mornin'. But about that Brisco, now. Never knew a feller who minded everyone else's business like he does. Always watchin' and thinkin'. Cozied up to them Millers who ran that wagon train that left town a few days ago. Didn't get nothin' outta them though. Oh, that Miller woman liked his flatterin' words all right, but she didn't let him near her wagon and them expensive doo-dads of hers. Them Millers were a right cagey pair. Thought for a minute he was gonna follow them, but he didn't. Musta changed his mind."

"No need to go after the Millers when I'm here," Rusty said ruefully. Ned gave a sharp bark of laughter.

"That Brisco sure got hisself a one-track mind. He won't let go of a notion until he sees it through. Been fellowin' you fer long?"

"A few days." Rusty rubbed his chin thoughtfully.

"If I was you, I'd just wait fer him behind a tree and let him have it. No need to wait to find out what he's gonna do. Plain to see. And you can take it from me that no one's gonna miss him," he assured him.

"A good idea," Rusty said regretfully, "but it isn't my way."

"But it's his way, boy! Just you mind that!" Ned warned. "No use wastin' any eddykit on that one. He won't appreciate it. You gotta hunt him like he's huntin' you."

"You're right," Rusty agreed. Another man came in to get his horse. He'd met Brisco too.

"Took him across river in my dugout and didn't even thank me. Just took to the hills when he got on the other side," he remembered. "Rude cuss. Didn't bother passin' the time of day with me. Just went off by hisself and paid no heed to us." The farmer was aggrieved. "And them eyes of his. They cut right through a body as if ya weren't even there!" He paused. "I didn't like him. Mind you, he didn't do me no harm. But, I don't know as I'd like to turn my back on him." Ned nodded in agreement.

"Took his shirts to Mrs. Blevins to wash." There was a dramatic pause. "He hit her!" Both men looked shocked. "Yes sir, said she wasn't doin' them right and he wasn't payin'. When she insisted, he slapped her 'crost the face. Then her husband come in with a gun and suggested that he not only pay his wife, but give her extry for the inconvenience. Well sir, he did!" the farmer said with relish. "Was that Brisco hoppin' mad!

The next time he brung her his shirts, she slammed the door in his face!" He smiled at that.

"Hittin' wimmin!" Ned shook his head. "That's bad. Do that to a woman, what'll he do to a man?" he asked, but his eyes were riveted on Rusty.

"Probably try to slit my throat," Rusty said cheerfully.

The farmer was impressed. He looked the younger man up and down. "Got it in for ya, does he? You be careful, young fella. He's the kind that keeps comin' and comin' if he's got ya in his sights. You be careful."

"I will," Rusty said seriously. Brisco seemed to make immediate impressions on everyone—always bad. Ned studied Rusty closely. He liked the young trader and didn't want to see anything happen to him.

"Got a plan?" he asked finally. The young man's face had become very thoughtful.

"I always have a plan," Rusty grinned. "I saw Brisco heading out of town—"

"There's some no-goods campin' nearby," Ned interrupted. "Probably knows them."

"Is that so? In that case"—Rusty stood up—"I'd better get going. I'm planning some entertainment for Brisco. It should keep him occupied for a while."

"If ya want to keep him occupied," Ned suggested, "hang him from a tree. That'll occupy him plenty."

By the time Rusty spoke to two more citizens he had a pretty good picture of the man he would have to deal with. For one thing, from the few people who actually associated with Brisco the general consensus was that he never seemed to do any work but he always had money or goods to trade. And money was scarce around here. Most folks just bartered goods for goods or services. Brisco would disappear for months at a time then show up at the tavern flush.

Both Joe and Lonny said Brisco wasn't much of a drinking man. He seemed to have contempt for those who were. Rusty wasn't a drinking man either. In his line of work a man had to be vigilant and alert all of the time. Drink only dimmed the senses. Brisco was probably disappointed to find that out.

By afternoon Rusty had ended up at the tavern where he had started. Joe Wilder was unloading some heavy casks from a wagon when he called out to Lonny for help. Seeing that Rusty was back, Lonny rushed over to help his pa. One of the casks was slipping out of Joe's grip and was about to land in the middle of the road. Rusty hurried over to give his friends a hand. Among the three of them, grunting and groaning, they managed to unload and carry the heavy casks into the tavern.

As Rusty straightened up again brushing dirt from his shirt, he caught a glimpse of movement in the stables. "Damn that prying bastard to everlasting hell!" he swore loudly. He couldn't leave his freight unguarded for a minute! So much for Brisco's great display of leaving town this morning!

Rifle in hand, Rusty moved quickly to the stables on cat's feet. He glanced around the door and saw Brisco hunkered down over his gear. He was peering closely at what was under the canvas cover. Even from here, he could hear Brisco's sharp intake of breath as he saw the silver. Then he reached out a greedy hand for it.

Moving soundlessly through the doorway, Rusty snapped his rifle to his shoulder, finding Brisco in his sights. The man was so immersed in what he was doing, he didn't recognize Rusty's presence until he heard the metallic click of the rifle being cocked.

"Get out or I'll blow you away!" The cold, hard voice sliced through the air.

Brisco stood up and turned to look into the frozen green eyes targeting him. Brisco's lips twitched. "Thought it was my pack, Rusty." Rusty felt a nervous shock course through him. The man had found out his name. He had tossed it off as if it was an obscenity.

Brisco saw that McBride had been taken aback so he pressed his advantage. "Need help hauling that silver, Rusty?" he asked familiarly. "How much do you have here? Plenty, I'd say. Now where would you be taking it I wonder? Fort Pitt? Of course. Where else would you be going with freight like that. You know, Rusty," the bold bastard continued, "it's a long trip for one man carrying so much silver. It gets mighty dangerous on the trail. A rough breed travels the mountain country. You should know that. You want to be extra careful . . ."

With a coolness that belied Rusty's state of mind he pulled the trigger. The rifle shot shattered the air. The acrid gun smoke swirled around in the stillness.

The bullet creased Brisco's shoulder. It sliced through his fancy white shirt, and a trickle of blood beaded the shredded fabric. He clamped his hand to his shoulder, his face a study in fury.

"I don't like threats, Brisco!" Rusty stated through clenched teeth. "You just mind your own business and you'll live longer yourself. You've had your warning, now get out!"

Face contorted, Brisco spat out, "If I were you, McBride, I'd be almighty afraid of not making it to Fort Pitt. I don't think you'll make it there. I've met a lot of men who were killed on the trail for their goods." Then he backed out of the doorway and disappeared around the corner.

Still smarting from the man's bare-faced arrogance, Rusty reached down to pull the cover back over his freight when something went flying through the air skimming past his head. He heard a sharp report and the sound of splintering wood. When he looked up, he saw a knife still vibrating, lodged deep in the stall plank above his head. If he hadn't ducked down just then, the blade would have struck his chest.

Livid, Rusty sprang to his feet and raced across the packed earth floor to the stable door. He looked around the stable yard and found nothing. Brisco had disappeared.

Chapter Four

Ben Allyn was more surprised than anything else when the handsome stranger he had seen in the tavern the other night turned up at his camp.

He skipped the small talk and spoke at once about why he was here. Ben thought that, although he was polite, the man didn't want to spend a minute longer here than he had to. It was all right with Ben. He didn't feel like company anyway.

"Heard you been having trouble with Kenny Minks." Ben blushed, ashamed to have a stranger overhear how he had been so stupid as to be duped by the likes of Minks. He didn't realize that was the very reason James Brisco was here. He needed a pigeon to pluck.

"Yes," he replied curtly. "But I'll get the money out

of him." Ben looked down at his bruised hands and the anger began to rise in him again.

"I got a beef with Minks as well." Brisco's words drew back Ben's attention. "Just been trading with the Shawnee. Got a lot of silver from them that I planned to take to Fort Pitt. A few days ago, Minks came up to me on the trail when I was camped and asked for a handout. He repaid me by stealing all my silver and goods. I got this from him too." Brisco touched his shoulder. His shirt looked bulky where a wad of cloth was bandaged to his wound. Ben saw an ugly gleam spark from Brisco's eyes. He knew Kenny Minks was a thief so he readily believed he had stolen this man's silver. Ben had not realized Minks was a killer too.

"He had me cornered, you see? And then he shot me. When I came to the next morning, everything was gone. I intend to track him and get that silver back." He paused. "I'm going to need a few good men to help me. How would you like to come along? I'll pay you one hundred dollars."

Ben stared. "One hundred dollars!" He badly needed the money. Ben thought about that piece of land on Saylor Creek and the cabin he wanted to build there. That hundred dollars and the money Minks owed him would set him up just fine.

"I got to get him, Allyn!" Brisco's low voice broke urgently into his thoughts as he saw the boy vacillating. "It will take more than one man to put him six feet under. It's a big job, but it has to be done right so he can't shoot or steal from any more law-abiding, honest citizens."

Brisco's hands shook and his eyes turned black like coals. His face was rigid. He sure was mad! The more he talked, the more Ben wondered at the man's almost fanatical hunt for justice. Maybe circumstances had fueled his state of mind. Ben knew that Minks brought out the worst in human nature. Ben had lost his temper too. Although, he had to admit, not like Brisco.

"All right, Mr. Brisco. It's a deal," Ben said reluctantly. Immediately after he agreed, he'd felt he had done the wrong thing. Deliberately, he pushed down the doubts that surged up. Maybe this Brisco had the right idea. He never let anyone push him around. Maybe Ben was too soft. Just complaining wouldn't get his money back. And he deserved it.

"Good, good!" The light died down in Brisco's eyes, and he relaxed. "I'll let you know when I locate him. Be ready to move out at a minute's notice."

And with that, Ben Allyn unknowingly threw in his lot with a very dangerous, very desperate killer.

Chapter Five

After his encounter with Brisco, Rusty was hungry. The young trader packed up his gear and stowed it in a dark corner to be loaded onto his horses at a moment's notice. After that, he went to the tavern to eat. He figured it would take Brisco some time to bandage his wound and change into another fancy shirt—probably take a good bit of time to curse out Rusty while he was at it. No need for him to go hungry while Brisco was busy. Rusty sat down to enjoy a plate of hotcakes.

"You all right, Rusty?" Joe inquired seriously.

"Well, I could use some more maple syrup," Rusty commented and poured a generous amount over his hot cakes.

"Don't like to bother a man who's enjoyin' his food as much as you are, but I been talkin' to Doug, the feller who runs the small trading post down the end of the road," Joe said apologetically.

Rusty nodded. "Met him."

Joe leaned closer. "He says that Brisco feller comes into the post this mornin' and wants to buy lots of ammunition. Enough to hold a fort."

Rusty's fork paused for a moment, then he continued eating.

"When he asked this Brisco what he wants all that for, he says he's got himself a snake to kill. Doug said he seemed to hate that snake almighty bad."

"Maybe the snake shot him in the shoulder," Rusty suggested.

"Durn it, Rusty, tain't no laughin' matter! You get six inches outta here and he'll jump you sure enough! 'Sides which, he got himself a couple of horses out at the Paxton farm. Old man Paxton's gettin' paid for keepin' 'em. This Brisco feller tole him it might be a week or two afore he comes back for them."

"That ought to give him time to kill me and take my silver, then come back for the horses," Rusty mused.

"Is that all you got to say?"

"Now that you mention it, no. Got any butter? It would be a damned shame eating Mrs. Wilder's excellent hotcakes without it."

Joe slapped a plate down on the table. "You know why he ain't takin' his horses? Easier to track a man on foot. You go by the same trail you always do and he'll find you right enough."

"I'm not intending to. I know a game trail to take. Not much to it, but I know it well. Brisco won't be able to follow me for long."

"How about if I come with you, Rusty? You could use another gun. Besides, I owe you."

Rusty smiled at his good friend. "No, Joe. You have a wife and son to look after. You'd be sorely missed if something happened. I don't have anyone waiting for me to return."

"It's too dangerous for just one man. Brisco ain't the only problem you're facin'. There's also them hostiles makin' bad medicine again."

"Joe, a man has to fight his own fights out here. I have done since I could tote a gun. I'm not putting my troubles onto your shoulders. I appreciate your offer, but no."

Joe was dejected, but he heard the resolve in Rusty's voice. Lonny came in, hands stuck deep down in his pockets. "It's almost time for them Virginia creepers to show up, Pa."

Rusty considered for a moment. Even though Brisco kept his whereabouts hidden, Rusty knew he would be back to keep an eye on him to make sure he didn't slip out at night without his knowledge. "You know, Joe, maybe there is something you could do. Do you think you could create a diversion? Then I can slip out when it's dark."

"Create a who?" Lonny asked.

Rusty grinned. "Get everyone in one place and keep them busy. Do you think they would show up for a shooting contest? They're popular at Fort Pitt. Men come in droves to compete."

"Shootin'! This ain't Fort Pitt. What the men like here is drinkin' and fightin' . . . and drinkin'."

"Joe, do you think you could announce a big drinking contest for this evening?" He pulled some coins from his pouch. "The first round is on the house. That should get everyone involved. After that, Jackson's men can pay since they'll be drinking the most. Then I'll slip out when everyone is busy."

"Hell, once they start drinkin', you can't get 'em away from it," Joe agreed. "It'll divert 'em."

By late afternoon Jackson and his men came helling into the tavern, slamming their backsides onto the heavy oaken seats. Jackson cringed, momentarily forgetting his injury from sitting down hard on the barn floor the other night. "Jumpin' cockerels!" he yelped, then settled down more easily, perching on the edge of the chair.

Joe Wilder studied Jackson's two black eyes and bruised lips. An angry cut split his high cheekbone. Joe hid his amusement poorly. He remembered that Rusty had delivered the one black eye, but he wondered where Jackson had picked up the other.

Jackson saw Wilder staring at his injuries and imagined he was impressed. "This is nothing! You should see the other man!"

"I seen the other man this mornin'," Joe returned dryly, "and he looked pretty damn good to me!"

Immediately Jackson's expression darkened, his eyebrows lowered menacingly. He opened his mouth to spew some choice backlash, but Joe cut him short.

"What about that drinkin' contest?" Joe asked him before Jackson could speak.

"Drinkin' contest?" he frowned. He groped around in his mind but came up empty.

"Don't ya remember?" Joe feigned astonishment. "Yesterday?"

Jackson put his hand to his head as if it would help his memory. "Drinkin' contest? That sure does sound familiar—'specially the drinkin' part."

"You said you and your men would take on all comers. Somethin' about defendin' the honor of Virginia from all them slights made yesterday."

"Yes, of course!" Now Jackson remembered. "A drinkin' contest! I remember!" He slammed his fist hard on the tabletop demanding silence of the boisterous crowd.

"Did you hear that, men?" he addressed his friends. "We're challenging every other man in this blessed settlement—if he is a man—"—he eyed the roomful of patrons doubtfully—"to step up and join me in a contest of nerves. To decide who the best man here is! Although I think you already know that! I think I settled that question last night!" The men looked at each other, nodding. They clapped, whistled and stomped their feet.

"Andy! Andy!" they hooted, pumping their fists into the air. He preened.

"I can't hear you!"

"Andy!" they shouted again.

Infused with excitement, Jackson hurtled across the room, jumped on a tabletop and planted his fists on his lean hips. "I declare here and now for all the world to hear, that my name is Andy Jackson and I can out-drink anyone within a hundred miles! Huh!" The men cheered wildly, apparently none remembering last night's debacle when their hero ended up in a horse trough.

"And just to get this here contest goin', the first round of drinks is on the house," Joe announced. There was an immediate swarming towards the counter as everyone rushed to get his tankard.

"Hold on! Hold on!" Jackson yelled at the top of his voice. They all stopped and looked. "I'm first! This here is my idea! Step aside there." He shoved one man who was in his way. The crowd parted and Andy waded up to the counter, slapping it for effect. "Give me one big pigeon, feathers and all!" he ordered. Joe poured the drink then Jackson put it to his mouth and sipped it reflectively. The crowd held its breath. He took another gulp, then he grinned. "That's danged good stuff. Give 'em all the same!"

The crowd cheered and surged forward grabbing for the free drinks. Joe and Lonny were hard-pressed to give them what they wanted. They all demanded it right away, some even trying to climb over the counter. Joe gave them a shove. "Wait yer turn, blast ya. You'll get yer drink!"

Meanwhile, Jackson plunked himself into a chair,

winced, then drank the whole tankard down, wiping his mouth on his sleeve. When he was finished, he called out, "Johnny! Donnie! Lonny! That's one. Give me another!" Since Joe and Lonny were too busy, Jackson merely got up and snatched the tankard out of the hands of an unwary patron. It was half full. "If you can't drink it faster than that, you don't deserve it," he declared and guzzled down the rest himself. He laughed at his own wit then looked about for any other laggards.

It was then that he spotted a pair of broad shoulders encased in buckskins, curling red-brown hair and a tall, lithe figure. By golly, it was purty boy! And he was drinking a mug of coffee! Andy almost retched. He suddenly remembered last night, how that man had sneaked up on him and beat him up! Andy felt outraged. He slinked over to his men who had gotten their free whiskey and were preparing to drink it at a table.

"Look who dast to come in here drinkin' coffee!" he hissed to them. They all turned to look at the offending figure sitting quietly by himself. They mumbled collectively in injured tones. "There he is . . . sore loser . . . cheat . . . dirty fighter . . . purty boy . . . white teeth."

The words drifted over to Rusty who, at first, paid them no mind. Finally fed up with it, he suddenly stood up, scraping his chair back. They gasped. Turning, he gave the men a menacing look. His angry green eyes bored into theirs. Everyone quickly shut up and avoided his eyes. They stared down into their drinks instead.

Deliberately, Rusty walked over to their table. For a

long moment he paused, standing directly behind Jackson's chair as if waiting for any of them to challenge him. No one did. Slowly he walked past them, even bumping a few chairs as he went by. None of the men objected. With one last penetrating look he turned on his heel and walked slowly to the door.

Rusty glanced back once more but no one said a word. All were hunched over, engrossed in their drinks. With a tiny scornful smile he pushed the door open and left.

The men finally looked up when he was safely outside. Now they didn't conceal their dislike. Damn him! Not a mark on that handsome face. They looked at Andy's beaten face. It wasn't fair, especially when Andy was the winner.

"Coward!" one man hissed although not too loudly. "Did ya see him a-skulkin' away?" he asked as Rusty's slim-hipped figure strode along the road that led to the stables. "No Virginia man would do that!"

The gang rose slowly to its feet. Jackson, seeing that his adversary had gone, shoved his way ahead of the others to get a better look at a real live coward. He spoke loud enough for the room to hear, but not so loud that it would carry to McBride.

"You come back here, you yeller dog! Ya hear me? Crawling away with your tail twixt your legs. Why, I'll throttle you and muzzle you myself here and now! Then I'll parade you around town on a leash. Ya hear me? Huh!"

"You tell him, Andy. Dirty sneak!" one man agreed in a low voice.

As Rusty kept walking, his easy, athletic stride took him past the tavern window. He nodded at Lucy, who sighed with admiration, devouring him with her eyes until he was out of sight.

"Shut that thar door!" Andy ordered and a half dozen obeyed. "So's I can give vent to my feelings without bein' interrupted!" After the door was safely closed Jackson proceeded to do so, interspersing his diatribe with as many insults as he could muster. When he was finished he rested, confident that he had come out looking the better man.

More drinks were dispensed. Not only Jackson's cohorts cluttered the inn, but others began arriving as well. "The place is startin' to look right festive," Joe Wilder enthused. "The news of them free drinks sure got around fast!" When there was a momentary break Lonny delivered the glad tidings to Rusty.

"The place is burstin' at the seams," Lonny informed the trader proudly. "They're even settin' out on the steps. Brisco ain't showed up yet, but more and more are passin' the word. Even them wild-eyed critters that camp down by the river is tricklin' up. From the way they act, you can tell some of 'em ain't looked civilization in the face for a considerable time."

"Good." Rusty grinned. "Even if Brisco doesn't show up for the free drinks, he won't be able to pass up an opportunity to relieve some of your esteemed patrons of their savings. Maybe he'll be so busy pilfering their pockets, he'll leave mine alone!"

"If he does, he'd better watch it." Lonny laughed. "A few of them specimens look right gnarly. They won't be easy pickin's." He saw Rusty was all packed. "You plannin' on leavin' now?"

"No, son. I'll sit in the doorway a bit. With luck, when Brisco arrives he'll think I'm settling down for the evening. Anyway, I'll wait till it gets a little darker so I won't be seen. Lonny, there's something I want you to do for me while I'm gone."

"Sure, Rusty. Anything."

"I want you to stay away from the stables. After I leave, don't come near the place until Brisco leaves Bewilderness."

"Why, Rusty?"

"It won't be safe for you, son. When Brisco sees what I left for him, he'll go berserk. I don't want you to get hurt. Will you promise me that, Lonny?"

"Sure, you can depend on me! I won't come any-wheres near here."

"Good. I'll feel easier in my mind now." He slipped Lonny a coin. "That's so you'll remember."

Whistling, Lonny went back to the tavern and helped his father serve more drinks. They exchanged knowing looks, and gave the customers what they ordered. At any rate, it was working, Joe thought admiringly. "The whole town must be here," he told his son and looked around, but—"Danged!" he swore, and Lonny looked at him questioningly. "Only one person missin' and it has to be that Brisco fella! Run and warn Rusty."

Lonny put the cup down and hastened outside. He was too late! The stables were empty and Rusty's horses gone. He ran to the other door but saw nothing. There was no way to tell which path Rusty had taken.

"Damn that Brisco!" Lonny swore softly to himself. He went back to tell his father who looked grim. "Let's hope he makes it all right." He was too busy to say more, but a worried expression played across his face all evening.

It was dark when Rusty led his packhorses from the stables. The muted shuffle of hooves moving through long grass was drowned out by the pandemonium coming from across the stable yard. Rusty circled the tavern giving it a wide berth. He stayed clear of the searching tavern lights that cast long shadows over the grass. The rising moon was obliterated by a cloud mass crowding up the sky. When he and his animals reached the tree line they merged with the darker wilderness.

Rusty traveled silently through the night, staying off the trail. A few hours before daylight, he pulled up at a small opening protected by thickets that backed up against a steep rock face. He unpacked and hobbled his horses and let them feed on the small patch of lush grass. Then he lay back and slept. Tomorrow would be a long day. He hoped Brisco enjoyed the drinking contest.

Chapter Six

When the wagon train stopped for the night, Aaron Fletcher could sit for only a few minutes on the horse's back waiting for the world to stop swimming around him. One part of his brain told him he ought to help Molly, but he was unable to move. It was only as people began to give him peculiar looks that he forced himself to stir from off the horse.

Molly, who had been watching with worry, ran over to help him dismount. She almost staggered as she took most of his weight on her arm. Aaron grabbed hold of the wagon to steady himself or he would have sprawled onto the ground. As he stood there catching his breath he turned his hands over. They were crisscrossed with red welts where he had hung on tightly to the reins during the day, afraid that if he'd loosen his grip, he would

58

topple from the horse. Automatically, he flexed his fingers to get the circulation going. He was aware of Molly's watchful eyes. He gave her a wan smile, which was all he could muster.

"Help me to the wagon, girl. I'm all done in." Molly did, her forehead puckered in a frown as he dragged himself into the wagon and lay down heavily. His eyes were dark and sunken behind his lids, and his skin flushed and hot.

"You just rest, Pa. I'll take care of everything," she said, spreading a blanket tenderly over him. He didn't even stir. She was bothered by his labored, uneven breathing. His fever was so high she had felt it through her cotton sleeve as her strong young arm had guided him to the wagon. Molly was afraid. Something told her that even after a night's sleep Pa wouldn't be able to manage the team. What would happen then?

Hastily, she started a fire and cut up some pieces of meat into an old blackened pot. Today, some of the men had gone hunting and brought back a deer. Game was scarce along the wagon trace so each family was given a small portion of the catch. She had heard the hunters' shots echoing in the far-off woods as they had made their way along. If she hadn't had her pa to fret over, she would have been concerned about how much noise they had made. Molly added some wild onions and a handful of corn to the stewpot. Pa had eaten nothing all day.

Afterward, she had hurried to lift down the wooden trough attached to the back of the wagon to feed the horses. As they ate, Molly returned to check on her father. He was sleeping, but not deeply or restfully.

Quietly, she pulled closed the back flaps to keep him from prying eyes. Molly had attached the flaps especially to keep the Millers from looking into their wagon. As head of the wagon train they felt it was their right to poke their heads into everyone's wagon to see what was in there. Once, Mr. Miller had looked in while young Mrs. Newsome was changing and she rapped him on the head with a cast-iron ladle. Mr. Miller didn't look in anymore. That didn't stop Mrs. Miller, however.

As Molly knelt by the fire a well-built woman about fortyish strode up. "Well, I see your father is not helping you," she pointed out without preamble. Molly knew Mrs. Miller would notice. "I can only come to one conclusion—he is unfit to help. Let me see him at once! I wish to judge for myself."

Molly jumped up angrily. "He's resting and you're not going to disturb him!"

Mrs. Miller abhorred the girl's defiance. In her opinion young girls, especially of inferior rank, ought to respect their betters. "I'm in charge of this wagon train and if he can't keep up—"

"We can keep up! We're here, aren't we? You have no cause to throw us out if we can keep up!"

At the sound of raised voices, other families left their wagons and came to gather around Molly Fletcher in support. They all liked Molly and her father. By contrast, they disliked and despised the Millers. All had observed how the Fletchers had been bullied by the two easterners. The other folks had done what they could to help, but it seemed it hadn't been enough.

"There she goes again! That she-devil is determined to get rid of her," one woman hissed to her husband under her breath.

The man looked puzzled. "You mean 'them.'"

"I mean her—Molly. That black-haired witch can't abide to see a pretty young girl like Molly around. It's been stuck in her craw since the first day."

It was plain to see that Mrs. Miller was becoming impatient with Molly's belligerence and the crowd's buzz of disapproval. She was used to giving an order and having it obeyed. This new country was a breeding ground for illiterate yokels who actually thought they possessed the same rights as the wealthy and educated!

"And what about tomorrow and the next day?" Mrs. Miller challenged the spirited girl. "The sicker your father becomes, the more it slows us down! I will not have it!"

"Let them be," old Mr. Kern intervened. "They've been keepin' up, and if they can't we can all lend a hand. Right, folks?" The crowd murmured in agreement.

Mr. Miller, who had come over when the commotion began, was leaning against a wagon watching his wife. She usually needed no help but now he took his cue from her. As he came forward, he saw the angry color come into Elvira's cheeks.

"You heard my wife. We're responsible for the welfare

of all the families," he began self-righteously, "and we can't let one drag us down." His intent was clearly to divide. It was the Fletchers or the rest of them. "All our families, our children, our wives," he gave them an artificially concerned smile, "will be put in more danger, not only because they can't keep up, but the fever could spread amongst us."

"Bull feathers!" Grandpa Kern replied. "You don't care about us, so don't pretend to. You just figger the more families travellin' with you, the safer your hide and your heifer's will be! Are we goin' to let these two fine people be left behind just because the Millers don't want to be bothered? Or," Grandpa added slyly, "is it because Aaron Fletcher has a pretty daughter?" The old man's keen eyes drilled into Mrs. Miller's and she read his crude disdain. The women sniggered.

Clem Miller felt as if he was losing control of them. He stepped in to try to pacify them before his wife exploded. He knew her well. "We all want to get to our new land as soon as possible. We can't do it if we're weighed down," he tried again.

"Let's have a vote," one man suggested mildly. The others liked the idea and there was a loud whisper of agreement among the settlers. Elvira was not about to let any vote take place. She knew very well what the outcome would be.

"There will be no vote," she announced stridently. "We're in charge here. We only let the Fletchers join out of the kindness of our hearts." Derisive snorts reached her ears, and her eyes turned hard, cold like ice. "And they should not have been permitted to come in the first place. Why do you think the other wagon train let them go? Because it was plain to see they were losing time as well." She tried to sound as reasonable as she could.

"We're not losing time," one man pointed out. "We're right on schedule."

"We had to stop early these past two days—"

"Because you were tired!" a feisty little woman with gray hair piped up. "Remember you fainted from the heat? Why don't you go back to the settlement?" There were hoots of laughter from everyone. "And don't tell us no claptrap like you stopped early out of consideration for the Fletchers!"

Grandpa Kern gave her an approving nod. "Atta girl!"

"One word from you, old man, and your whole family can leave as well!" Clem Miller moved towards him threateningly.

Young Mr. Kern stepped out in front of his father, rifle in hand, a stern look in his pale blue eyes. "You just keep your temper, Miller, and don't be threatening anyone, or you'll catch hell. From me!"

Miller stopped. He swallowed hard. He could browbeat the old coot, but the younger Kern was not a man to trifle with. He was a dead shot with that rifle of his. It would be extremely foolish to mark him as an enemy. The people had suddenly quieted around him. How quickly the temper of the crowd had changed. He could feel their dislike. Miller knew his options. He could either push it or back down as diplomatically as he could.

"I was merely trying to make a point," he said coldly.

"Well, mister, you just stand right over there whilst you're a-makin' it," the younger Kern suggested.

Miller, sensing he was losing control, was silent. Mrs. Miller, however, was not ready to give up. Kern wouldn't threaten a woman. Anyway, she wanted those two out and she wanted it done now! It was plain to see her husband was not the person to do it. Suddenly she turned on Molly.

"Let me see your father. I can judge then!" She started to walk boldly towards the wagon.

Mr. Fletcher had awoke from his uneasy sleep. He had heard the piercing voice of Mrs. Miller and the deep, arrogant voice of her husband. He knew everything had come to a head. He wouldn't let Molly face it alone. Using every bit of his strength, he finally managed to shed his blanket and pull himself up into a sitting position. He was just about to pull the wagon flap aside when it was yanked open. He found himself staring into the black, infuriated eyes of Mrs. Miller. For once she was taken aback.

"Mrs. Miller," he said in a slow but deep voice. She backed up and Molly hurried over to help her father down. Although it cost him all his effort, he remained erect, his head high as he confronted those two.

"Well, Mr. Fletcher," Elvira accused in her harsh voice, "I can see that you are worse than before. We have no alternative but to let you go on your own way.

You are no longer a part of this wagon train." Though she spoke to Mr. Fletcher, she was looking spitefully at Molly as she said it. She had the pleasure of seeing the girl pale with fear and anger.

"We didn't have a vote!" Mr. Kern pointed out loudly. "And I vote we let them stay."

"I second it," another one said. "And I." All voices were raised in support of the Fletchers. Sick as he was, Aaron was warmed by their loyalty. He also saw the fury in the Millers' faces. At that point, even though he didn't want to, Aaron knew he could not keep up nor could he ask these good people to help him. He was a proud man.

"Thank you, everyone," he said sincerely. "I surely do thank you for stickin' up for Molly and me. I can't say how grateful we both are for your support and friendship, but for once the Millers are right." He barely gave the couple a glance. He sighed heavily. "I can't keep up and it wouldn't be right to make you fine folks help us. We should have stayed back at the settlement until I was better. But when I am, we're comin' to Fort Pitt and I'll look forward to having you all as neighbors." He slid his eyes at the Millers.

"All except you. I never said this before to a livin' being, but now is the time to do it. I never met up with such hardness and selfishness in a pair as you two. In this country people help each other. You'd better learn that because, believe it or not, one of these days you might have to depend on the very people you hold in contempt. And they won't be there to help you." There were nods of agreement from the crowd.

"Out here we don't care about a person's rank or money or friends. We look at that person and see if he deserves our respect. And you two"—his eyes went around the camp—"haven't earned the respect of a single body here. So you can keep eatin' off them china plates if you want." This caused a titter of amusement that made Elvira even madder. "But it don't impress us one bit. Because inside, you're both no-account cowards and bullies. And—" Aaron stopped and looked around at all the sympathetic, kindly faces. They had been through a lot together. "That's all I have to say except good-bye. I hope you all make it safely. God bless you."

Molly, seeing that he was spent from his emotional outburst, rushed to his side and put her arm around his waist. Grandpa Kern stomped over boldly and, ignoring the Millers' scowling faces, helped Aaron back into the wagon again.

"Thanks, Mol," her father whispered. "I feel like I been dragged fifty miles. I should have shut up and not been so long-winded."

"You did good," Grandpa Kern encouraged him. "Never did see a female look so mad in my life. And you know her. She's always het up about somethin'."

"I think she's going to say something," Molly said to Mr. Kern as she pulled the flap down and turned with him to face the Millers.

"Yep," Grandpa whispered to her. "Jezabel speaks!

Think she'll bust a blood vessel, her face bein' so purple-like?"

Mrs. Miller's face was indeed purple-like. Mr. Fletcher's speech about them was the final straw. Her temper reached a new height.

"You're leaving now!" she ordered Molly. "Not to-morrow! Now! Get your wagon out of here, out of sight of this camp!"

"Now hold on here!" Grandpa shouted, outraged.

"Don't worry, Mr. Kern," Molly said with more calmness than she felt. "We're not going anywhere."

"Damned right!" he agreed.

"Unless the two of them want to hitch themselves up to our wagon and pull it out of camp!"

"Like a matching pair of jackasses!" Grandpa hooted, slapping his knee.

Mr. Miller came forward as if to grab hold of Molly's arm and force her out. Suddenly, he realized to his chagrin that the girl was holding a rifle in a most businesslike manner. Its muzzle was pointed at him.

"Get back, Mr. Miller. I'll shoot you if you make any more trouble for us! And you too, Mrs. Miller," she added, seeing the woman start toward the Fletcher wagon. "This is not your woods and we can camp where we like." They both saw the hardness in her usually soft brown eyes. Neither had an understanding of people, nor did they wish to. They were keenly aware, though, that the crowd had turned ugly. Their antagonism was palpable. Mr. Miller had a feeling that if he tried to forcibly remove the Fletchers there would be blood shed. And he had a pretty good idea that it would be his own.

As he halted in his tracks, Mrs. Miller overbearingly prompted her husband. "Clem!" Clem ignored it. He saw that some men had rifles and they all seemed to be pointing at him. He was naked and vulnerable without his weapon.

"Very well," he tried to sound cool, as if he was still in control. "We'll let them stay."

"Mighty good of you," Grandpa Kern snickered. It had the effect of riling Mrs. Miller.

"Clem, I want you to get them out!"

"Oh, let them stay," he snapped, then turned on his heel and stalked away, leaving his wife staring after him, open-mouthed. She looked about her. For the first time she realized that she was alone and that the faces watching her were unfriendly. A fearful tremor tingled up her spine. She hesitated, then she lifted her head.

"Very well, they can stay for tonight only," she stated as if she were a queen granting a reprieve, then stomped away after her husband.

Well, it had happened, Molly thought. The thing she had dreaded most had come to pass. Now what were they to do? More important, what was she to do? One minute, they were members of this train, and there was safety in numbers. Now she would be thrown to the mercy of every disaster that could threaten a woman alone in this empty land. Panic seized her. How could she handle the wagon by herself? She wasn't even sure she could find her way back to the settlement. And then there were the hostiles! Her heart felt faint when she thought about it.

She shied from asking the final question of herself: What if Pa died? What then?

Molly barely heard the people as they came up to her. To a man, they were all sympathy. Some even urged her to come with them anyway, or at least follow their trail. Then, when her pa got better she could catch up.

Molly nodded, but she had seen how sick Pa was. It was farther to the fort than it was back to the settlement. Considering she had to do all of the driving, she thought it was wiser to go back. Besides, Molly didn't know what the Millers' reaction would be. Right now, they were both incensed. Clem Miller might take it into his head to break a wheel or do something else destructive to prevent them from catching up. She had seen him examining the spokes one day when she had gone to fetch water from the stream. Molly knew in her bones that if she hadn't come back quickly, he would have damaged the wheel in some way.

So when she thanked everyone sincerely, Molly told them her mind was set.

"I don't want to bring down trouble on anyone's head," she said earnestly. They all thought it was a shame and tried to help her in any way they could. Though they had pitifully little themselves, the settlers shared what they had. One woman brought some bread over, another one had her children fill up the water barrels on the side of the Fletcher wagon. The men gathered around and examined the wagon thoroughly, looking for anything that needed to be mended before the two were left to endure on their own.

"Let me make that brake a mite easier to handle," one man told her. By the time everyone had left Molly was confident that everything on the wagon was in good working order. With tears in her eyes she thanked them all, assuring them that she and her father would be fine. They knew she lied, but they all pretended to believe her.

"Maybe we should have George go with her," Mr. Kern said to his wife, speaking of their fourteen-year-old son. "Then he could come to the fort with the next train comin' out. I hate to think of that little girl handlin' that big wagon and horses all by herself."

Mrs. Kern bit her lip. "I'd like to help, John, but"—she paused—"you and I know that those two will probably never make it, what with the Indians and all." She started to cry. "I don't want George to be kilt along with them. I like Molly and her father, but you know we'd never see him again." Mr. Kern sighed. He thought that with George along, the two might have a better chance, but his wife was right. George was just a boy, after all, and certainly not as much help as they needed.

"There, there." He patted his wife's shoulder. "You're right. I just thought . . ."

Grandpa Kern voiced their frustration in three words. "Them damn Millers!" Then he stomped off to feed the horses.

All evening people kept stopping by to ask if the Fletchers needed anything. Everyone came but the Millers. They sat off by themselves eating and drinking, quite pleased with themselves.

Towards dusk, as Molly sat silently by the fire, something tapped her lightly on the shoulder. She glanced up in time to see a small pebble drop onto the ground. She looked about but saw no one. Shrugging, Molly lapsed back into worried thought. Then another pebble hit her, this time on the hand. As she turned, a small one landed in her hair.

"Ouch!" she said, more from surprise than because it hurt her.

"I'm sorry," a hollow little voice reached her ears. It seemed to come from the bushes. As Molly watched, two blue eyes peeked out through the foliage. They darted about to see if Molly was alone and anyone was looking. Then a little girl of about six came crawling out, headfirst.

"Shhh!" she whispered nervously. "I don't want anyone to know I'm here." Molly recognized her. It was the little blond-haired girl that the Millers had working for them. They worked the pitiful little creature shamefully.

"Come here. I got something for you," she beckoned excitedly. Molly got up and went over to her, kneeling by the bushes.

"What is it?"

"I heard you have to leave. The Millers are so mean! But I borrowed something for your father." Her hand, dirty from crouching on the ground, produced a small box. "Here, it's restorative tea. Some doctor mixed it up for ailing old folks so it must be powerful good. And your pa is old. Mrs. Miller says it'll cure anything. And here's some pork jelly. That's supposed to be good for you too. She swears by that. She swears about a lot of things. Give it to your father, but please don't tell anyone that I gave it to you."

"Did you take these from the Millers?" she asked, surprised and alarmed.

"Yes, but they won't never miss them. They have well nigh a ton of useless stuff in their wagon."

"I don't think I should—"

"They're already took, and it will be harder to put them back," she said practically.

Molly smiled, touched by the little girl's concern. "Thank you. I'll give them to my father. I'm sure they will help him."

The little girl beamed happily. Molly noticed how terribly thin she was. Before the girl could leave she said quickly, "Let me give you something in return. Mrs. Carter just gave me a fresh loaf of bread. I'll cut you a piece." The little girl's blue eyes brightened as she waited for that. She accepted the thick slice eagerly and bit right into it. She didn't even let the crumbs get away, but dabbed them up with her finger. Molly guessed she wasn't fed very well by the Millers.

"Thank you." She swallowed it down and smiled. "It's good. And I'm hungry. Mrs. Miller wouldn't give me anything to eat today because I spilled her perfume. I was only sniffing it, it smelled so pretty."

When a step sounded behind her, the little girl vanished quickly into the woods. A bit of brown calico streaked across the clearing in the distance. That's right. Molly remembered that the Millers made the child look after their prize cow. She had to lead it well away from the campsite. Mrs. Miller was very sensitive to the smell of the animal. Molly turned, but it was only Grandpa Kern asking her if she needed help lifting her father.

That evening, several of the families tried to talk to the Millers, hoping that time and reflection might have changed their perspective on the Fletchers. Mrs. Miller was pleased to announce that they hadn't.

"Well," Mrs. Miller said, coming up to Molly the next morning and smiling coldly at the girl, "I hope you two make it back to Bewilderness all right," she lied smoothly in front of the others. Now that she had gotten her way, she was her sweet self again.

"I'm sure we will," Molly returned shortly. Rudely, she turned away to bid a warm good-bye to all of the new friends she had made.

Mrs. Miller didn't care. She had won. Now she waltzed back to her wagon, contented.

After breakfast, a forlorn Molly watched as the wagons were hitched up and moved out. Ignoring Mrs. Miller's triumphant smile and Mr. Miller's piercing, unfriendly glare, Molly waved as the wagons rumbled past her.

Too soon, they were out of sight. As they rounded the

bend in the track, Molly's eyes filled with tears. She blinked them back. At the end of the procession she saw a small, shabby figure leading a cow. She turned and waved. Molly waved back. Maybe she was the luckier one after all.

"Everything all right, Mol?" Mr. Fletcher asked heavily as he ate his breakfast. "I'll get up in a minute."

"No need to, Pa, the men are helping," Molly said firmly. Relieved, he fell back into a deep feverish sleep.

With reluctance, she packed up the rest of their belongings. Well, no use putting it off, Molly told herself as she climbed up onto the wagon seat. Indecisiveness was not exactly a sin, but it was no virtue either. Molly squared her shoulders and took up the reins. Their lives were in her hands now. She hoped she was doing the right thing.

The Fletcher wagon rattled along the rutted track for a while, then Molly left it and headed across fields and meadows. They were heading back to Bewilderness. Molly didn't know if she could make it there all by herself. She wasn't even sure if she was headed in the right direction, but she was going to try.

Her small hands grasped the reins tightly. The wagon heaved and creaked over the broken ground. Just a few days, that's all she needed. A few more days and they'd be safe back at the settlement. Would they live through those days?

Chapter Seven

Lonny Wilder knew his father was worried about Rusty, so he decided to do something about it himself. He gathered together his two friends, Billy and Riley, and unveiled his plan.

"Now, Rusty said I wasn't to go near the stables with that Brisco fella in town. But why shouldn't I?" he asked his two friends. "Ain't them our stables?" The two boys agreed seriously that they were. "And why should I be afeared to be agoin' on our own property jest 'cause a that scowlin' wretch?" The two boys agreed that that was hardly fair.

"What right does that Brisco fella got ta keep ya away from the comfort of yer own stables?" Riley asked.

"If ya want to lay abed in yer own hayloft, what's it got to do with him?" Billy put in.

"If ya want to go a-pattin' yer horses or jest settin' in the shade of yer own roof, what's it got to do with him?" Riley added.

"I won't be chased outta my own stables!" Lonny nodded. "And you two won't neither!" They both expressed gratification. "Now I've been a thinkin' hard, and I don't like the way Rusty had to leave town in a hurry jest 'cause that varmint was eye'n up his silver."

"Thievin' skunk," Riley muttered.

"And what do we do with thievin' skunks?" Lonny demanded. The boys had no idea but were willing to hear any suggestions. "We trick 'em, that's what we do!" he declared, hitting his fist in his hand. The boys looked interested. He was finally on familiar ground. "Yes sir. Rusty wanted that Brisco critter to think he's still in town, but if I know that varmint, he'll be a creepin' around here and trying to see for hisself. He did it when Rusty was in plain view in the light a day, and ain't nothin' gonna stop him now." He paused dramatically. "'Cept us. See here?" He showed them a gold coin. "Rusty give it to me to help him and I'll share it with ya." They looked eager. "All we got to do is pretend that Rusty is still here. That way, old Brisco will lolly around town and Rusty will have plenty of time to get to Fort Pitt. What do ya think?"

"You must be a genius 'cause that's a plumb good idea," Riley agreed. Billy nodded as well. "Have ya got yerself a plan?"

"Course I have. Tonight, when that snake comes a

slitherin' around, we'll be waitin' fer him," Lonnie said triumphantly. The two other boys exchanged looks.

"Ya mean ya want us to shoot him?"

"I can git my pa's gun," Riley volunteered handsomely. "He always leaves it about when he's drunk."

"No, I mean we'll fool him into thinkin' I'm Rusty!"

Billy looked at him. "He won't be much fooled lessen he's blind in both eyes and stupid in his head. You ain't of a size."

"I will be covered up in my blanket with jest a mite a my haid a showin'. He'll think it's Rusty sleepin' here."

The boys looked impressed with the brilliance of this idea and agreed to meet later that day with the necessary things.

"But I'll bring my pa's gun just the same," Riley said, and Billy agreed to bring his too. "Best to have a gun handy in case things don't work out. That's what my pa always says: Cold steel is sometimes better'n cold logic."

"That thar is somethin' to remember." Lonny nodded solemnly. "Amen!" Billy added virtuously.

All day long, Riley, Lonny, and Billy took turns hanging around the stables. Every time Brisco approached, they grabbed up their rifles, stared at him knowingly, and took precise aim. The looks he shot at them would have been enough to curdle milk.

"Pay him no nevermind, men," Lonny urged them, much as a general would instruct his troops.

The boys had seen where Rusty had taken some old

packs and tucked them away in the hay. He had allowed just enough of the packs to show through the wisps of hay so that a sharp-eyed skulker like Brisco would be sure to spot them. He would think that Rusty had hidden his silver there, then paid the boys to guard it. The boys laughed that Rusty had tricked him good. They saw with unholy amusement that Rusty's estimation of Brisco's character was correct.

"Brisco will think he's real clever, spotting these packs in the hay," Rusty had told Lonny.

That was exactly what Brisco thought. Brisco figured that the boys, moving about in the stable, had loosened some of the hay, exposing the packs of silver. That's what comes of enlisting the help of young whelps, Brisco mused.

That night he planned on stealing the packs. His lips curled in what was meant to be a smile that distorted his handsome face. He pleasurably considered how he would outsmart McBride. Did he really think a few half-grown boys would scare him off? Brisco's fingers caressed the blade of his tomahawk as his eyes fixed on the stable door.

Tonight he would get it. He wouldn't need Farley and Lem after all, but he thought he'd have that Ben boy meet him out of town. He could help him transport the silver. He'd be a good drudge to have along. The boy was honest and wouldn't think of stealing from him, which was more than he could say about Farley and Lem. Yes, he was honest, Brisco smiled scornfully, which is to say stupid. Anyone who would go after Kenny Minks and take only his wages was, in his book, a blockhead. Still, he was a useful blockhead—until his use was over. Then he would become a dead blockhead, because Brisco had no intention of sharing his money with anyone—not even one hundred dollars' worth.

"Did you see him a-lookin' where the packs are hidden?" Lonny grinned to the boys when Brisco moved off. "Rusty was right. He fell for it. Thinks them packs are full a silver!" All three had a good laugh at Brisco's expense.

"You watch, though," Riley said, taking up a piece of straw and sucking on it. "He'll be back tonight. Jest grubbin' fer that silver. Mark my words, now."

"It don't take no prophet to know that. Any man with two eyes in his haid can figger it out," Billy said.

"Well he won't get it. We'll do jest like we planned to do. The longer we keep him a guessin' the longer he'll stay about town. When he sees me a lyin' there pretendin' ta be Rusty, he'll be plumb scared outta his socks." Then he added, "If he wears 'em."

Billy jumped up. "There's only two kinds of men in this here world—them that wear socks and them that don't. Brisco now, he certain sure wears socks, 'cause my ma did his washin' fer him, and darnin' too. He's mighty particular 'bout them shirts. Them that are perticular about shirts is particular about socks too," he said wisely. Lonny and Riley nodded in total agreement. "Here! Here!"

"I betcha he comes a-tiptoein' in here tonight in his clean, darned socks to get that thar silver." They all laughed as Billy imitated a hunched up Brisco prancing over to the packs.

"Shhhh!" Riley went over and stuck his head out of the door. "He's skedaddled now. Goin' towards the woods. Bet he's plannin' somethin'." He had an idea. "Why don't I follow him?"

"Best not," Lonny said regretfully. "You don't want to track that he-coon. Never know what he'll do if you corner him far from the settlement. Best jest do what Rusty said. 'Sides, what good would it do ya? Ya can't warn Rusty."

Riley agreed with great reluctance. He enjoyed making sport of the likes of Brisco, who had hit Billy's mother. Still, tonight they'd fool him good.

That evening, the boys met at the stables eager to carry out their plan. "I know what I'm doin'," Lonny assured his friends as he rolled up in the blanket. "There. How's that? Billy? Riley?"

"You need a mite more bulk. You stuff some of that hay under that thar blanket. Rusty has big shoulders. Yer lookin' a bit flimsy."

"Flimsy?" Lonny sat up, letting the blanket slip. "That's turtle twaddle!"

"What ya gettin' so huffy about? Look at them bony shoulders!"

Lonny flexed his scrawny muscles. "Look at that. That's from heftin' kegs of whiskey!"

"They sure don't amount to much," Riley said critically. "My ol' granny has more muscles than that! Now you jest do what I say." Lonny stuffed hay around the upper part of his body underneath the blanket. "How's that?"

"A lot better. Yer lookin' more like a man should."

"I think he needs a bigger haid," Billy added. "All that stuffin' 'round his shoulders and now his haid don't seem right."

"Billy, yer pate is plumb addled. Go sit down somewheres and don't be doin' no thinkin'."

"But it still ain't right, Riley," Billy pointed out. "His legs is too short."

"By golly yer right! I knew it! I plumb knew it! That's why I brung my pa's boots. We'll stick 'em under the bottom edge of that thar blanket. It'll add two feet to his height at least." Riley arranged the blanket over the boots, then stood up to admire the total effect. "It's a thing of beauty." Then Riley warned Lonny, "It weren't easy gitten them boots offen Pa's feet, drunk or sober. If he finds I took 'em, he'll flay the hide offen me. So you be good to them boots. Treat 'em like yer own mother. And when the shootin' starts toss 'em outta the way."

Riley tucked the blanket around Lonny and gave it one more look. "Looks fine," Billy approved.

"Now lookee here. Billy and me will be hidin' right here in the corn bin, a hairsbreadth behind ya, with our rifles trained on this Brisco feller. But you keep yer gun to hand anyway. You understand, Lonny?"

"All right."

Riley and Billy, aged twelve and thirteen, climbed into the corn bin and watched the doorway through the slats in the bin wall. Both boys meant business. Billy's pugnacious young face was set in a scowl. Riley was cool and calculating and opinionated. He was running the show. They would wait here until Brisco showed up, even if it took the whole durned night, Riley swore solemnly.

Time passed as they sat peering through the darkness at the stable door. After a while, their legs began to cramp and their eyes drooped. They began to figure that he wasn't coming after all. But just when they thought he wouldn't show, a long form materialized in the open doorway. A dark shadow stretched eerily across the hard earth floor, making the boys draw a quick breath. It was Brisco. He stood silently there, gazing at the sleeping form on the other side of the vast interior. Lonny froze.

Riley warned, "Watch it, boys, we got ourselves a bear. I got his tail bacon in my sights." Lonny tried to control his accelerated breathing. Meanwhile, Billy and Riley hunkered down, barrels raised and level with Brisco's chest. Both boys watched him through the slats with eyes filled with fearful eagerness.

From behind him, Riley coached Lonny. "Lonny, let the light shine on them brass fixins on yer rifle. That'll cool his innards. Keep yer finger near the trigger. Keep up the scare."

Lonny shifted his gun slightly so that the tavern light lit on the brass trim of his rifle. For a fleeting moment as he stood there, Brisco considered killing McBride here and now as he slept. There were no witnesses around. Then he saw McBride's finger near the trigger of his rifle as the tavern light glinted on the brasswork. Even in sleep, he was a careful bastard!

Riley's voice whispered to Lonny again, "He's a thinkin'. Show him the kind a man ya are. Snore! Make them rafters rattle!" Lonny gave it a try. It came out a little weak, then picked up in volume.

As Brisco watched from the doorway, he thought about the ambush site he had chosen a little way out of Bewilderness. On second thought, it would be safer to kill him out there on the trail. There would be no tavern owner to come running to help him then. The man had too many friends here anyway. He smiled in the darkness. If McBride only knew how close he had come to being a dead man! But Brisco could wait. He backed out and melted into the night. Lonny whispered, "Is he gone?"

"Yeah!" The two boys came out into the open, rifles in hand.

Lonny threw off the blanket and sat up. "Thanks a lot, men."

"That's all right, Lonny. I'm jest waitin' fer my chance to be McBride. I'm feelin' a little bit sleepy myself. We can keep this up all night." Riley added, "That was a real slick idea of yers, Lonny. You shoulda seen his face. He thought he had ya dead in the sack. Don't know what made him draw back, lessen the sight of you was so fearsome." The three boys laughed softly.

"If my pa knowed what I was doin', he'd be madder than a he-goat."

"I'm glad Brisco took outta here, for his sake. There might a been murder done tonight," Billy said sagely.

"Yeah, to you," Riley taunted.

"Nahuh."

"Oh yeah."

"Stop it, you two," Lonny scolded. "That sneakin' polecat might take a notion to come back."

"Don't you worry, Lonny. He durst not. I seen his face. He was a smirkin' and a grinnin' like a skunk that found itself a mess of grubs."

"Mebbe so, Riley, but we'd best stay all night. Cain't never tell what's a goin' on in his haid. 'Cept it's nothin' good!"

"All right by me," Riley said, sitting down again in the hay. "Long as I can git them boots back on Pa's feet afore he comes to."

Rusty awoke suddenly in the darkness. All his senses were alert. Everything around him was still. He looked to where his horses stood and saw they had their heads up. Their attention was drawn to where the trail wound below them.

Rusty rolled soundlessly to his feet, then moved quietly to look around. He saw nothing. After a while, his horses settled down and continued to crop the grass. The danger was past. He sat awake for the rest of the night listening.

The eastern sky was graying when Rusty loaded up. Then he hiked down to the trail, searching for signs of who had passed in the night. As daylight filtered through the overhanging trees down to the trail below, he saw the wagon ruts made by the train up ahead. There was no sign of anyone else. Rusty hesitated for a moment, then followed in their tracks.

Chapter Eight

Tonight Molly would stand guard over the wagon again. After a few days' travel her pa was feeling a little better, but not well enough to leave his bed. Rifle in hand, tomahawk at her side, she huddled down in a thicket where she had an unobstructed view of the camp. Since leaving the train, the threat of an Indian attack preyed on her mind—especially at night when they were most vulnerable. She didn't know exactly what she could do if many of them came at her, but she would do her damnedest to fight them off.

Molly's hand went down to the knife in her pocket. One old Indian fighter once told her if she was ever taken by hostiles, she should slit her wrists. She shuddered.

"Sounds bad, I know," he told her, "but I've seen what they do to captives and the women are treated as bad as the men. You take my advice, girl, and do it." After a long pause he said, "I wish my wife had done it. I had to bury her." He shook his head even though it had happened almost fifteen years ago. "I'm givin' you good advice. Kill yourself afore they do. It'll be quicker."

Molly pushed these gruesome thoughts from her. She doubted she would do it anyway. Leaning her cheek against her rifle, she looked out at the pitch-dark surroundings. The moon was on the wane and there was very little light. That was all to the good. There was less chance of being detected.

A rustle sounded near her. Silently, she slid her rifle to her shoulder and peered into the shadowy bulk of forest. From somewhere behind her she heard another furtive noise. In the dim light Molly could make out a doe and her fawn poised there watching. They were dark outlines against the blacker night. For a long time the doe observed Molly closely then, nudging her fawn, the two moved off slowly foraging for food.

Molly let out the deep breath she had been holding and brought her rifle to rest on her knees. After that, there was more bustling about as opossums and raccoons went about their nocturnal ramblings. She had learned to recognize the various sounds and no longer jumped at the flurry of wings or the creeping of tiny feet. For three hours she watched until fatigue finally overcame her and she nodded off.

The side of her face rested against the rough bark of

a maple. Her bright hair, stuffed into an old hat of her father's, didn't show at all.

About an hour later, three dark figures came past the camp not twenty feet away. They did not see the wagon hidden by branches or the girl guarding it with her rifle. The moon was too pale and weak. Besides, they were on the trail of something big. They did not think to look for further sport when they had a more tempting quarry in sight.

Luckily for Molly, she did not hear them approach nor did she see them vanish in the same direction the wagon train was headed. Sighing a little in her sleep, she rested her shoulder more comfortably against the tree trunk and did not open her eyes until it got light.

Molly awoke with a start. The cold, damp air of the night had seeped into her cotton dress, chilling her. Some guard she was, she thought as she shivered. Her small hand touched her face gingerly where it had rested against the rough bark. Her legs were cramped, but Molly remained still from habit.

The eerie sounds of the night were gone, to be replaced by the busy, cheerful scurryings of squirrels. The birds sang as the warm sun came up disbursing the shadows and making the world a safe place again. Nothing intruded on the pleasant scene. Smiling at a raccoon who was climbing back up his tree after a late night, Molly padded over to the wagon and looked in.

Her father was still sleeping but, even to her critical

eye, he seemed to be better. His breathing was not as labored. She touched his cheek. His skin didn't burn as it had the last few days.

Aaron awoke at the touch. "Mornin', Molly." He yawned. "Cold, isn't it, for such a sunny day?" He pulled the blanket closer.

"Are you?" She sounded pleased. "I'm glad." At his look of surprise she said, "It means your fever is not as high."

"You'll be happy to know then, that I'm not warm." Molly smiled at the gruff words.

"I've got some bread left and some jelly. Then I'll brew more of that restorative tea for you. That should brace you up."

"You don't have to, Molly."

"You need something warm in you."

"It is warm," he admitted grumpily. "But that's about all you can say about it. Where did you get that tea from, anyway—the creek bed?"

"You're close. I got it from Mrs. Miller," she said airily, not telling him exactly how she acquired it.

"No wonder it tastes so bitter. That's probably why she gave it to you. One way to get rid of it."

"Probably," she agreed. "I'll be back, Pa. I need some wood."

"Don't make too big a fire and don't get no green wood. It smokes too much." She nodded, then moved off. In a short while she had a fire going.

"Here, Pa." Molly handed him the tea carefully in a mug. "I'd like to make a warm meal, but I hate to have the fire going too long—"

"Where is everybody, Molly?" her father interrupted, taking the tea and craning to look past her. She lowered the flap a little. "Just busy, Pa," she evaded.

"I didn't see anyone last night, Molly," he said sternly. "Why hasn't anyone called on me? Where is Grandpa Kern? Why is it so quiet?" When she was silent, he said, "If you don't tell me, I'll just get up and take a look myself." To prove this, he started to push away the blanket.

"Pa, don't! I didn't want to tell you because, well, you must have forgotten. But"—she swallowed hard, picking her words carefully—"don't you remember how the Millers threw us off the wagon train? You thanked everyone and told the Millers what you thought of them."

"Did I, Mol?" He leaned back, sighing. "I've had so many bad dreams about the Millers, I guess I plumb forgot what was real and what wasn't. Come to think on it, I do remember. I guess it wasn't a dream." He slanted his sharp eyes at her. "How long have we been on our own? Now tell the truth, girl. I can't abide bein' coddled."

"Just a few days," she assured him. He looked at her slim shoulders and small hands.

"And you led the horses all that way yourself? I don't know how you did it, Mol, but I'll be helping you today."

"No you won't. I can do it. I have done it. Besides, I don't want you dying on me—at least not until we get to a settlement."

There was a glimmer of humor in his eyes. "I ain't gonna die, child. This fever's taken hold of me good, but it'll pass. Soon as I have this tea." He paused. "Did you say the Millers gave it to you?"

"Don't ask so many questions, Pa. Just drink the tea."

"Molly, I know you'd never steal a pin from anyone, but where did you get the tea?"

"Someone gave it to me. Now, that's all I can tell you except that it's from the Millers."

"What if they claim we stole it? We could go to jail, and they'd do it too! That witch-woman would bring her own mother up before the magistrate!"

"We have bigger things to fret about, Pa, like getting back to civilization so we can be put into jail."

"You're right. I don't like borrowing trouble. After I have my breakfast I'll lend you a hand, Molly."

"No you won't—now that's an order! It'll be just like last time. You getting better, working a spell then getting sicker again. I can do it! Maybe later on you can help, but not now." Unwillingly, Aaron settled back. He was feeling a bit better but he was exhausted. He didn't think he could be of much help to Molly anyway. He'd probably make more work for her than she already had. Abhorring his helplessness, he lay down. His head was beginning to get muzzy again just from talking.

Chapter Nine

That evening, Lonny, Billy, and Riley readied themselves again. "Let's git goin'," Lonny urged, "afore that
thar Brisco comes a weaselin' around."

"Here." Billy crammed more hay into the sleeves of
Lonny's shirt which had too much stuffing already. Tonight, Lonny was wearing one of his pa's shirt. It held a
lot of straw and it bagged down almost to his knees
where it was tied to hold in the stuffing.

Riley looked at him critically. "It looks like ya got
the gout in yer arms, they're so big." Then he dropped
his pa's boots to the ground—his pa was drunk again—
and went over to Lonny. "Here. Let me show ya how
it's done." He fluffed up the hay-filled sleeves until
Lonny's arms looked like huge turkey wings. "That's
better," he giggled.

"I'm a he-man!" Lonny swaggered across the stable, so stuffed with hay that he crinkled with every movement. Then he threw back his head and crowed like a rooster.

"Yer one fearsome sight," Billy hooted.

Lonny strutted around, then came to a stop in front of them, thickly padded legs spread as far as they could stretch. He placed his hands on his hips, his huge arms sticking out like oversized handles, and declared in a loud voice, "My name is Rusty McBride and I can lick any thievin' weasel within a hundred miles a here, and that includes James P, as in polecat, Brisco, huh!" The boys laughed uproariously as Lonny minced about, putting on a show for them. The hay that was stuffed into his pants began to bag up into his seat, then sagged downwards.

Billy jumped to his feet, hands clasped together. Trembling, he begged Lonny, "I know I'm a mean ornery, low-down skunk, but I cain't help it. Please don't hurt this worthless mullet, Mr. McBride, sir," he groveled.

"I'll think about it, old loon. Well, I thought about it. I've decided that I'm gonna beat ya down until ya fit into a lard bucket. Then people will know ya fer what ya are." Hands still on his hips, Lonny strutted deliberately towards him, emphasizing each word as he stepped closer, "Yer a big. Low-down. Thievin'. Pig-stealin'. Silver-stealin'. Cur. And I'm the man to teach ya a lesson, Brisco!" He stomped his boots loudly at each word. Both boys went off into peals of laughter.

Billy sank to his knees and begged, "Please, O Great One! Please don't beat me into a bucket of lard!"

"Well," Lonny said. "All right, then. Rise, Sir Mullet, and don't ya never show yer ugly face around these parts agin!"

Immersed in laughter, a grinning Lonny turned towards the door, hands still on hips, all ready to strut the other way. His grin froze when he saw the cold-eyed anger of James Brisco!

"Arrggh!" Lonny's high-pitched scream shocked the boys.

"What the hell's going on here?" Brisco snarled, his eyes going to the packs. Deciding that prudence was the better part of valor, the boys sprang up like they were sitting on a hot griddle. They headed en masse for the back door.

"Come on, Lonny!" Billy yelled as Lonny, stuffed with hay, shambled as quickly as he could towards the open door. Brisco made a snatch at the trundling boy, but came up with a handful of straw, which he flung to the floor furiously. He cursed the retreating rear soundly.

"Don't forgit Pa's boots!" Riley screamed. Billy dived in front of Brisco, grabbed the boots, and scrambled off after his friends into the darkening night.

As he tried to squeeze out the narrow opening, Lonny's over-crammed butt got caught in the partly opened door. He was going to get caught! The boy shoved the door wildly with his fists, then whacked it open with his inflated behind by banging it back and forth. As he lumbered after his friends, his hanging rear slapped against the back of his knees, impeding his forward progress.

Riley glanced back and watched in horror as Lonny's pants began to slide over his slim hips. He yelled, "Lonny! Grab the seat of yer britches! Yer leavin' a trail of hay even that polecat can follow!"

Riley hurried back to Lonny and hoisted up his pants, propelling the boy ahead of him. "Hustle yer hocks, son! He might foller us yet!"

"Do ya," Billy gasped, tired from carrying both the boots and the rifle. "Do ya think he found out yet that them saddlebags is filled with rocks?"

"No," Lonny said, sweating from so much hay in his clothes. "And I don't wanna be around when he does!"

The boys didn't stop until they were in Riley's cabin where they locked the door and fell onto the floor.

"Thought ya said you were gonna pepper his tail," Lonny said to Riley.

"I coulda, if you'd jest laid down and not gone a-prancin' all around the place and callin' Brisco down on our haids."

"I'm surprised he didn't pepper yer bottom, Lonny," Billy remarked. "It was hangin' low enough!"

Lonny removed the offending hay and his body resumed its normal proportions. He pulled off his britches and shook them out. "That stuff itches like the devil!"

"Ought we to go back an' do somethin'?" Billy hissed, afraid even from this distance, that Brisco might hear.

"Like what? Get ourselves kilt?" Riley asked practically. "It's too late now, anyhow. Once he finds them rocks, he'll be on the warpath. It's best fer us jest to lay low. We'll let Rusty send him to glory."

Lonny stood up. "Well, men, it looks like our work here is done." They shook hands all around solemnly.

Brisco strode into the stable, watching the boys take off through the other door. What were those three pups doing in here making sport of him? His mouth hardened. He'd like to take a strap to them! And where the hell was that bastard, McBride? It appeared he was fool enough to have them guard his silver. That's what came of being soft and trusting in boy recruits. No doubt McBride was hiding in the woods hoping Brisco would be stupid enough to follow his false trail in an attempt to lead him away from his real stash. A simple plan and worthy of the dull-witted McBrides of this world. Brisco sneered at his unworthy adversary. Here was the silver right in his grasp. Meanwhile, McBride was waiting in the cold, damp woods wondering why Brisco hadn't turned up yet.

The irony of it pleased his arrogant soul. Now it was time for the payoff. He grinned at his easy victory. Striding purposefully towards the packs, barely discernible to any but those with the sharpest of eyes, he kneeled down. Greedily, he dragged them out from under the hay. There were four of them—each filled with silver! Yes sir, this was James' lucky day, all right! And it wasn't costing him a single bullet.

They were certainly heavy enough, he thought, grunting from exertion. Old Rusty had been holding out on him. There must be plenty of silver here. More than even he had calculated!

Hands shaking with barely restrained excitement, Brisco tugged at the straps holding together the first pack. The straps stuck and Brisco clawed at the canvas futilely. In anxious frustration he drew his scalping knife, then plunged the blade into the pack, slashing it to ribbons. With a muted exclamation, he finally sliced through the leather straps and pulled open the flap.

He dug his hands in and pulled out . . . a handful of small rocks. For a full minute, all Brisco could do was stare stupidly at them. Then a flurry of anger mounted his cheeks. It had to be a trick! McBride must have put rocks on top, hoping he'd look no further. After all, McBride had seen him nosing around his freight. Brisco scrabbled in the pack, but turned up nothing except more stones and rocks.

Finally, in a paroxysm of outrage, he grasped the bottom of the sack in both hands and upended it. Rocks came tumbling out onto the floor. And more rocks. Brisco was stunned, then he steadied himself. McBride must have put this one dummy sack here, but surely the others were real.

He opened all of the packs but the same result met

his eyes: nothing but piles of stone, dirt, and rocks. Every one of them! The significance of what McBride had done finally sank in. He threw the worthless packs down, swearing loudly and profusely. There were not enough words to describe the intensity of his rage with McBride, but he managed to do it justice.

But Brisco was still unwilling to believe that the young, naive-looking trader had planned this all out beforehand. He refused to entertain the idea that McBride had guessed Brisco's intentions and left, taking the silver with him.

It must still be here. His eyes darted around the stable. They alighted on the horses. That was it! He had probably hidden the silver with the horses! It was then that Brisco made the unhappy discovery that McBride's horses were no longer there. The stables at the end where he had tied them now housed other animals.

Brisco exploded. "When I get hold of you, McBride, I'll kill ya!"

Glaring about in rage, he searched for something, anything, to destroy. He savagely slashed sacks of oats and grain, then kicked the bags over, scattering the contents over the ground. In uncontrollable fury, he picked up an empty barrel and hurled it through the air. It bumped along the earthen floor, bounced off the door, and rolled out into the yard and smashed loudly against a tree. Spitting out a poisonous string of oaths, Brisco ransacked the stable.

His frenzied emotions finally spent, he collapsed

against the stable wall. He'd get McBride! He'd get
him if he had to hunt him to Fort Pitt and back again!
But he'd get him and hack him into little pieces! His
hand reached down to his tomahawk. He hadn't used it
in a while. He'd get to use it now.

"What the hell are ya doin' here?"

Brisco spun around. He found himself looking down
the barrel of a rifle. Joe Wilder was at the other end of it,
face stiff with anger, brows drawn together in puzzled
offense. He had his gun trained on Brisco as if he was a
cornered wildcat. He saw the unnerving look in Brisco's
eyes. His shirt was pulled out and torn at the elbows. His
hair, usually immaculate, was messy and falling over his
sweaty, filthy forehead. His chest pumped up and down
as if he'd been running for miles. Joe looked at him
doubtfully. He took a tighter grip on his rifle.

Everyone came running out to see what the hoopla
was about. The three boys crept out of the cabin and
down the road to see what they had wrought. Even
Andy Jackson put down his cup to follow the others
outside into the yard. Excitement like this didn't happen all of the time! They crowded behind Joe Wilder,
amazed at the sorry sight of James Brisco.

"Jumpin' cockerels!" Andy exclaimed, looking at the
spectacle from behind the safety of Wilder's broad
shoulders. "That thar man is madder than ten pigs with
only one bucket of swill!"

Mrs. Wilder shook her head in horror at the damage
and she urged her husband to action.

"I want you outta here—now!" Joe ordered, confounded by the man's mad behavior. "If'n I see you agin, yer a dead man. Now git!"

Brisco stared at Wilder, then at the three boys taking cover behind the big man. Their faces were blank with innocence as they watched him.

Brisco reached instinctively for his knife, which he had dropped on the floor.

"Leave it!" Joe shot out, his usually genial face glowering. Brisco straightened. For a full minute, he stared at Joe as if debating whether he'd really shoot. He looked at the older man's face and decided to pass on it. With an oath, he walked out of the door, shouldering his way through the small crowd that had joined with Wilder to see what all the ruckus was about.

"And don't come back!" Riley hissed confidently as Brisco passed him.

Brisco spun around and raised his hand to cuff the boy across the mouth. Then he heard Wilder cock his rifle. He dropped his hand. Balling his fists at his side in suppressed anger, he stalked off. The crowd dissipated.

"Pa, look at this place," Lonny said, stepping in past his father to better see the destruction. Lonny went over to one of the packs and held it aloft. It hung in the air, limp and shredded. "Looks like it was mauled by a cinnamon bear."

"Bear, nothin'! It looks like he chawed it up himself, he was so danged mad!" Riley added colorfully, now that the danger was past. The boys giggled at the image it conjured up. Joe Wilder looked at the boys suspiciously.

"Lonny, you know anything about this ruckus?"

"No, Pa! How could ya think such a thing?" Lonny proclaimed in outraged innocence. "We didn't have nothin' to do with Brisco goin' hog-wild."

Joe looked at Billy's face and then at Riley's. Without blinking an eye, they both stared woodenly back at him.

"Hmm. I wish I could believe you. But you boys put things right here and I won't say another word—for now."

"All right, Pa," Lonny agreed readily, glad to get off so easily.

"Sure, Mr. Wilder," Riley consented without any argument. Joe gave them a look that clearly said that he didn't believe them, but he handed them his rifle. "Just in case Brisco is a slow learner. You boys watch out." With one last look, he headed back to the tavern. The men were waiting for their drinks. No one objected to Joe ordering Brisco out of the settlement.

"Nothin' slow about Brisco," Lonny voiced his opinion when his father had safely left.

"Now as to that, I jest don't know. Lookee how long it took him to figure out that Rusty left? Two whole days!" Riley boasted. "That's one more day than Rusty thought he could fool him."

"Did ya see him rip up them packs? Like a crazy beast!" Billy pounced on one of the sacks and took it between his teeth, shaking it heartily. Straw flew over his head.

"Yeah. And we drove him to it," Lonny pointed out with pride.

"That's right, we did!" Riley looked much struck at this revelation. "'Course, he was daft to begin with," he admitted. "Cain't take too much credit."

"He's plumb gone over the edge," Billy said gleefully. "And now he'll probably take off after Rusty." The boys suddenly looked stricken.

"Do ya, do ya think Rusty can handle a wild man?" Riley asked worriedly.

Lonny at first looked guilty, then said more heartily than he felt, "'Course he can! Did I ever tell ya the time that Rusty kilt fifty Injuns? I didn't? Well, I'll tell ya now . . ."

Chapter Ten

Rusty stood on a small crag and looked restlessly back over his trail. Frankly, he was puzzled. Two days and not a sign of Brisco. Surely those packs he'd placed under the hay hadn't fooled him for very long! Perhaps, Rusty speculated, he hadn't had time to examine the packs yet. After all, Bewilderness was a popular stopping place, a haven for fugitives as well as law-abiding citizens. Others may have taken refuge in the stables. Maybe some salty types that Brisco was giving wide berth to.

He hoped Joe Wilder hadn't had any trouble with him. When Brisco discovered Rusty gone, he might just think he could force Joe to tell him his whereabouts. Rusty smiled wryly. Many people made the mistake of thinking Joe an easy target. That is, until he walloped them with his club. He liked to keep an assortment of them behind the bar. There was a length and thickness to match Joe's every mood. Brisco, Rusty pondered amusingly, would no doubt be treated to the hefty board.

Rusty once again turned his study to the landscape. He felt pretty confident that as of now, he hadn't been discovered. That might not last long, but while it did he tried to put in as many hours of travel as the horses could take.

He knew Brisco would be upon him soon. That was inevitable. Of course, Brisco might not be as expert a tracker as he was a thief. The one thing he did possess, however, was persistence. Rusty remembered how Brisco's eyes had glittered with greed when he'd pulled up the flap and seen all that silver. He would be coming, all right. Rusty raked his fingers through his hair and turned to his horses. What the hell! Let him come on after him! He'd be ready for him and anyone else!

"Come on, girl," he patted the nearest horse. "Time to be ambling along." He didn't press his animals but kept a steady pace that got them further than if he'd tired them out by hurrying. Keeping his horses in good shape was more important to him than rushing around. They carried heavy loads and needed constant rests.

Rusty was in luck. Since leaving Bewilderness, he'd been following in the tracks of the wagon train. The churned-up trail made it impossible for anyone behind him to distinguish his tracks from all the others. That would buy him more time. He figured a few more days and he would peel off somewhere so that anyone following would not suspect it or be watching for it.

This plan was quickly abandoned the next day. In fact, all thoughts of Brisco were soon replaced by another, more proximate danger. Rusty pulled his horses off the trail and went over to study some new marks. His face tightened as he saw the prints emerging from the woods and blending with the tracks left by the passing wagon train.

McBride swore out loud. They were being followed. He squatted down and studied the ground. About twenty to twenty-five bucks were on their tail, he reckoned. It was a war party all right. There were no women or children along and they were traveling fast. They had the settlers in their sights. He only hoped those folks in the wagons weren't green and were aware of who was trailing them.

Rusty sincerely doubted it though. From the prints he had been reading, they were mighty careless. There was evidence of people wandering far from camp, some of them women and some alone. Children too. He'd seen where one small pair of feet was leading a cow into a meadow out of sight of the camp.

He stood up, disgusted with their recklessness. One thing they didn't seem to do was post guards or scout the territory before or behind them. They rode blithely on wearing blinkers. They wouldn't stand a chance against this raiding party. The skilled fighters would overwhelm them if given any chance, and it was apparent they were giving them plenty of chances.

Didn't they know they were a prime target? Some of

those wagons were weighed down with women's goods and furniture. No matter that the horses would be exhausted hauling such loads or that they would never be able to outrun their enemy. Probably they were newcomers to the wilderness. Rusty scowled. He had enough trouble looking after his own hide. Now he would have to worry about them!

When he got to their next camp, he couldn't believe what he saw. A small barrel shot to bits. Target practice! His jaw hardened. The noise from that would echo for miles. It was also a flagrant waste of lead, and they would need that ammunition! Damn those fools! He turned abruptly away and started off. Not that he had any hope of catching up to them and giving warning. They were too far ahead. Besides, he couldn't move fast enough. Not with horses weighed down with the heavy silver. He knew with cold certainty exactly what he would find anyway. The next morning, he came upon them.

The night before, he had made camp early, not wanting to run into the war party himself. Nerves strained, he wondered as he made his coffee, what time of day the wagon train would be attacked. Probably now, when they were most vulnerable, bone tired after a day of grueling travel. Now, when all a body wants to do is rest. It would happen while they were making camp, strolling around, dozing, getting supper ready. He could feel icy tendrils of apprehension creep about him. He knew it would be soon. No need to wait.

Even while he sat here sipping his coffee, they might

be fighting for their lives. The coffee left a bitter taste in his mouth. He tossed it onto the ground and rolled up in his blanket.

Nothing to do but wait and see. Nothing, he told himself sternly. The gnawing agony of helplessness robbed him of his rest. As he got up in the damp, gray dawn the uneasy feeling was still with him. Not bothering to make any coffee, he merely chewed on some jerky as he packed. Slowly, cautiously, Rusty followed the cold trail. Somehow he knew it didn't matter anymore.

It was the sound of flies he heard first. A consistent, annoying buzzing that got louder and louder as he approached. Cresting a ridge he saw the tops of the wagons. They were still smoldering. A stiff breeze brought the acrid smell of burned wood, ashes and char to his nostrils.

From the summit he surveyed the scene. The settlers had camped last night in an open meadow. With the thick trees and undergrowth all around them, the Indians took them completely by surprise, firing upon them with little danger of being targets themselves. The attack came suddenly. After the first savage volley, they rushed in for the kill. The annihilation was swift and complete. Rusty had enough encounters with them to know that.

For more than an hour, Rusty crouched there studying the camp then slowly circled it. It looked as if the hostiles were gone. Still, you never knew about Indians. Hunkered down, he waited a half hour more, his legs stiff from staying motionless.

Massacres, particularly of women and children,

revolted him no matter how many he had seen. And he had seen his share. The killings were bad enough but the torture and mutilations that preceded them ate at his guts. Rusty had seen hardened mountain men, no stranger to death, sicken at the cruel inventiveness of the savage mind.

These folks now, had not put up much of a fight. Chances were, from what he'd noticed, many of them had been caught without rifles when the attack came. Rusty avoided looking at the torched wagons where several bodies lay, heads bloody where scalps had been torn off. Not even the children were spared. One woman had made a run for it into the woods. Gently, Rusty covered her up. Dead or not, he didn't want anyone else to see what they had done to her. He found the body of a child underneath a bush where he had crawled to hide. The boy had been struck violently with a tomahawk.

Rusty's stomach clenched as he took on the grim work of checking for survivors. When he was done, he leaned against a tree and gulped in some sweet, clean air from upwind.

They had been thoroughly butchered. Things had been tossed carelessly out of the wagons as the Indians had looted them. As he stood there surveying the carnage, a colored object caught his eye. He picked it up. It was a child's doll. About to drop it back on the ground, he instead tucked it into his pack. Some little girl had loved it. Be a shame to let some Indian burn it if they should return.

When he reached the next settlement, he'd let them know what had happened. They would send a burial party to do the decent thing. Maybe notify kin. There were times he had done burial duty. It was a grisly job, but he'd like to think someone would do the same for him.

Despite his need to move out fast, the tall, dark trader still found time to cover all of the bodies in whatever cloth he could find. It was the last act of kindness these people would receive. At last, in the afternoon, he circled back to make sure no Indians were on his trail. Then, satisfied, he continued on, starkly aware of the danger ahead of him.

It was about a mile from the massacre that he heard a noise. Startled, he stopped in his tracks to listen. For a long time there was nothing. There it was again! A scuffling sound like rustling leaves. His green eyes slowly scanned the woods. Another noise and his eyes were riveted to his right. It was from there, he was sure, that the sound issued. His glance finally settled on a big, fallen tree covered with moss and half rotted. If someone was hiding, it would be here.

Slowly he shifted his rifle, that never left his hand, until it was pointing in that direction. He let go of his lead horse who stood obediently in one place. Soundlessly for such a tall man, he crept closer to the tree. He heard scratching as if something was burrowing further under the log. It could be just an animal but it made too much noise for that.

Watching closely, Rusty worked his way around the

tree until he could see the other side. It sure as hell was no animal! A scornful smile lifted one corner of his mouth as he saw the awkward movement. His rifle slid down to aim directly at whoever it was. If it was an Indian he was about to go straight to hell or wherever they figured they were heading on these momentous occasions.

"Don't shoot! It's only me!" A high-pitched voice trembled in the air. Rusty's expectant smile vanished and was replaced with an astonished look. A little girl climbed out from underneath the log. She was all dirty with dried leaves clinging to her long blond hair. She looked to be about six years old.

"Gosh, mister, I'm so glad to see you. I thought I was the only one." Her big blue eyes filled with tears that she knuckled away with a grubby little fist. "I heard the Indians. I heard the noises but I was too afraid to go back. I had to feed Bessie, the cow, see?"

The little girl with the cow. Yes, he saw. He nodded gravely.

"I ran and ran until I came here and crawled under the log." She lowered her voice to a terrified whisper, her little body shuddering as she spoke. "I heard them. At night. I think they were looking for me. They looked an awful long time. I thought they were going to find me but they didn't."

"That was a smart thing to do," Rusty said calmly. "Many adults wouldn't have thought of that."

"Are . . . is everyone . . . gone?" She gulped.

"Yes, I'm afraid everyone is gone." His face was somber. "Were your folks back there?" he asked kindly.

"No, my parents died of the fever and I was going to stay with my Aunt Charlotte near Fort Pitt."

"Then you'd better come along with me." He leaned down and lifted her over the tree. She was no weight at all. She seemed pleased at the idea.

"My name is Rusty McBride. I'm a trader taking my goods to Fort Pitt."

"My name is"—she paused a moment—"Isabelle. Isabelle Trelawney." As he set her on the ground, Rusty wondered at the pause but said nothing.

"I knew an Ichabod Trelawney—"

"It's not him," Isabelle assured him quickly. She was hurrying to keep up with his longer strides. He shortened them when he saw how out of breath she had become.

"Do you think, maybe, we could go get Bessie?" she asked shyly.

"I somehow think Bessie won't be there," he said tactfully, knowing how Indians senselessly killed livestock as well. When he looked at her worried little face, he relented. "I'll go back to see, but I don't expect to find her." He did find her, though. Unaware of what had happened to her owners, Bessie was munching contentedly in a lush meadow. Taking up the rope, he led her along. Milk cows were worth money. Maybe the aunt and uncle would be glad for her, especially with a small child.

"Bessie!" Isabelle exclaimed rapturously, trying to hug the placid animal around its neck. "I'm so glad Bessie is all right!" She beamed, her small face suddenly pretty. "Now I won't be so alone. Bessie has been here since we started. I used to take her out to find a field every night."

"I know," Rusty agreed sternly. "It was a stupid thing to do, sending you out all alone like that with Indians around. Those people didn't have much sense."

"That was Mr. and Mrs. Miller. They were very rich. They made me take Bessie out. They said no one would dare attack them. Mrs. Miller's family is well known . . ."

Fools! Out loud he said, "We'd better be on our way. The Indians might decide to come back."

"Can I hold your hand?" Her little face was hopeful.

Rusty shook his head. "Best not, Isabelle. I've got to lead my animals with one hand and hold my rifle with the other. Besides, we'll go faster if you ride." He set her astride Blackie. Her thin legs dangled down on each side, barely straddling the animal's back.

"I can ride the horse?" She seemed awed. "I never got to ride before. I always had to walk."

"Tell me something that will surprise me," Rusty muttered as he led them out.

"Now, you hold on tight and keep your eyes open— and your mouth shut," he warned as she opened it to speak. She seemed like a talker. Normally, he wouldn't mind. "We don't want to attract the Indians or anyone else." His green eyes swept the landscape as he spoke.

"Yes, Mr. McBride," she said obediently. "But who else would be following?"

"You'd be surprised. I got a hunch I picked up a couple of varmints since I left the settlement. Figure they're still around. Anyways, best to act as if they were. So listen. And watch. And call me Rusty," he added with a grin.

Isabelle liked the grin. She smiled back, showing dimples. "I will, Rusty." True to her word, she kept silent and kept swinging around in the saddle looking for "varmints."

Leading them through the woods, McBride stayed alert for any unusual noises. They moved slowly, avoiding large stretches of open meadow and keeping to the dark woods when possible.

Rusty didn't like the situation in which he now found himself. He knew when he packed so much silver there was the outside chance he might run into an occasional thief. He also knew he'd have to keep an eye out for the Indians. What he didn't expect was picking up someone like James Brisco. A dedicated thief, he had "found" Rusty at the settlement and was no doubt clinging to his trail. Probably, Brisco picked up a few cutthroats along the way. How many and what manner of men they were occupied Rusty's thoughts. Had Brisco brought along one more? Two? Three? More than that and Brisco couldn't handle them, Rusty figured. Moreover, he didn't think there was more than one Brisco in the mix. Brisco would be smart enough not to hire someone too much like himself. That would be courting trouble.

Then there were the Indians. The massacre of the whole wagon train had been brutally unexpected. A few bucks raising hell might have picked off a couple of settlers and maybe run off some horses, but a war party of over twenty was something he'd bet even the colonel at the fort didn't know about.

He would have to be on his guard day and night. All the more so because of Isabelle. That was something else he disliked. Laying his own life on the line for his freight was one thing, but this little girl depended on him to take her safely to the fort. She needed some luck in her life and, unfortunately, Rusty was it. He didn't like to think what would happen to her if Brisco got hold of her. It was a tossup which would be worse for the girl, the Indians or Brisco. He was here to make sure neither found her.

Any which way he threw the dice it was bad. Rusty hoped the massacre would occupy Brisco for a while. A scavenger like him couldn't resist stealing from the dead. But Rusty knew, however, that no matter what crossed his path Brisco would keep on coming after him. That silver would be uppermost in his mind. He wouldn't rest until he cut Rusty off before he reached the fort. Here was a problem Rusty would have to think about. Already, he was considering several plans to decrease Brisco's numbers.

Rusty glanced back to see how Isabelle was doing.

Poor little mite, there wasn't much to her. It was clear she'd been neglected. He remembered that her parents had just died, but her sad condition was certainly not recent. Her scrawniness was long-term. Whoever her parents had been, they had not done much to improve her lot in life.

Maybe they had been indentured servants from the old country. People like that were coming over all the time. Locked into a caste system in England where they and their children had no hope to better themselves, they came flocking to America. It might take them years to work off their debt but at least when they had, they were free to labor for themselves. In England, hard work didn't guarantee anything—except that your landlord got more profit.

When they camped that night, Rusty rummaged around in his pack until he found what he was looking for: a piece of soap, some clean cloths, and an extra hairbrush.

"Isabelle," he called. She came quickly. "Here." He handed them to her. "One cloth to wash with and one to dry." She was overcome by such largesse, especially when he said she could keep them for herself. The Millers had never given her anything.

"I'll wash myself every day! They won't go to waste." Still pouring out her thanks, he pointed her in the direction of a small stream.

"Make sure you wash your face real good," Rusty warned. "It's a bit gray looking." Isabelle strictly obeyed.

She came back with face and hands scrubbed and her hair neatly brushed. It was long golden hair and should have been tied back with a ribbon. The best Rusty could do was a piece of string. She took it as she took everything else, with a grateful smile.

While she had been washing, Rusty had gotten a meal together. Isabelle sat down and watched as he dished out the food. "Think you can handle this much bacon and beans?" he asked her as he handed her a loaded plate.

"I can eat that easy," she informed him. And she did. She ate, Rusty noticed with a touch of anger, as if she'd been starved. Despite her small size, she managed to consume everything on the plate before Rusty even got halfway through his.

"I'm pretty full," he lied. "Think you can get down this other biscuit?"

"Mm-hmm." She nodded, reaching for it eagerly. "You sure are a good cook, Rusty," she said thickly, downing the last crumb and licking her fingers to make sure she got every last bit. It was probably the biggest meal she ever ate, he guessed. After swallowing the last mouthful she leaned back contentedly, at peace with the world. She was now ready to indulge in an after-dinner tête-a-tête.

"Are you married?" she ventured.

"No, not yet," he replied, not a bit put out by his single state, it appeared.

"Couldn't you find a girl? That should be easy for you!"

"I've been keeping my eyes open."

"What kind are you lookin' for? Maybe I know some."

"Well, let's see. She has to be beautiful, and well-read, and intelligent, and sweet-tempered, and know how to knit and weave and tan hides." He warmed to the subject. "And build a cabin, and sew, and mend a wheel and shoe horses."

"Is that all?" Isabelle asked, staring at him.

"Well, there are a few more things, but that will do to start with. So what about it, Little Bit? Know any women who can do all those things?"

"No," she said sadly.

"Too bad," he said cheerfully. "I would've married her in a flash."

"Couldn't you just settle for her being pretty and nice? Do all them other things matter?"

"Of course!" he pretended surprise. "Why, who would fix my wheel if it broke on me? Who'd shoe my horses?"

"A blacksmith?"

"Why pay a blacksmith when you can get your wife to do it?"

She looked at Rusty and saw the twinkle in his eyes. "Gosh, Rusty, I thought you meant it." She heaved a sigh of relief. "You would never let a girl fix a wheel."

"Only if she did it well. I'm very particular about my wagon," he said, but she knew him well enough now to know he was funning.

"I knew a real pretty girl in Boston," Isabelle offered handsomely.

"Yes?" Rusty looked up interested.

"Real pretty. Long black hair, blue eyes and a trim waist. That's what the men used to say, 'trim waist.' Men seemed to like trim waists."

"It doesn't hurt," he admitted.

"And all the men were courting her. They would bring her bouquets and things most every day," she confided.

"And did this paragon get married?"

"I don't know what religion she is but she's not married yet. I bet she'd marry you lickety-split!"

"Why is that?"

"'Cause she can't cook. But you don't mind that, do you?"

"How do you know she can't cook?"

"Well, I don't know exactly, leastways I've only heard the men talkin' about her. They say that her pancakes taste just like horse blankets." Rusty tried not to smile. "So she always keeps a big pitcher of molasses on the table to pour over them."

"Man cannot live on horse blankets alone, even if they're covered with molasses. Well, I'd better wash those dishes." She jumped up to help him. As she did, he looked sideways at her.

Although he had no knowledge of women's things, it struck him that she was mighty shabbily dressed. The calico dress she wore was a depressing snuff-colored affair. It hung loosely on her skinny shoulders. At the waist it was secured with a piece of rope because it was so long. Not only that, but her moccasins were old and worn and ready to fall to pieces. Well, at least he could take care of that. After he packed away the utensils he took out a piece of rawhide.

"Here, Little Bit, plant your foot right there." She did and he cut it out. Her eyes were big.

"What are you doing?"

"Making you some new mocassins. Yours are about worn out."

"New mocassins for me?" She was estatic.

"Can't think why the Millers, if they were so rich, didn't give you a decent pair to wear."

"Mrs. Miller said she wasn't going to use her money to buy me anything. That I should be grateful that she was even allowing me to come along and eat their food."

"She sounds like a lovely person," Rusty grunted, cutting strips.

"She was very pretty and she had lots of dresses, some of them were silk!" she sighed longingly.

"How did you come to be with them?"

"The lawyer, Mr. Jenkins, paid them to take me to Fort Pitt."

She then went on to describe her home in Boston, which to hear her talk, was a mansion filled with servants. Her parents were rich, she claimed. And she had lots of clothes, books and jewelry and everything else she could think of. Rusty glanced at her threadbare clothes. The only thing he believed was that her parents had died of the fever. He was going to ask her where all her millions were when her father died, but he didn't want to put her imagination to the test. It had been a long day.

She refused to sleep until Rusty had finished the moccasins. When he had, she put them on and pranced about.

"I love them, Rusty! They're so soft and warm and comfortable! My feet always got cut in the other ones. Thank you!" She threw her arms around his neck and gave him a fierce hug. Rusty blushed but was pleased she liked them so much. No doubt he was elevated in her eyes to equal Bessie.

"These are the nicest things anyone ever gave me!"

"Nicer than those silk dresses you left behind in Boston?"

"Nicer, because you made them just for me." She blinked back tears of happiness.

Rusty was embarrassed. He wasn't used to female tears. "I'm glad you like them. Now go to bed and get some sleep. We'll be moving out early."

Rusty wished he could sleep as soundly as Isabelle. But from then on, he acted as if they were the hunted and he hated it. He hated the feeling of not knowing when or where. Soon he would have to make his move, and it had better be before Brisco did.

Chapter Eleven

"**G**et up!" Brisco's foot slammed into the sleeping man's blanketed body. "Get up! Both of you!"

"Umph!" A black-haired man shook his shaggy head and sat up slowly. "What the hell! What's wrong with you, Brisco? What time is it? Cain't a man git any sleep?"

The slimmer man jumped to his feet before Brisco's foot could land in his side. "What is it, Brisco? What's happening?"

"He left!" Brisco ground out through clenched teeth. "McBride's left!"

Lem wasn't as surprised as Brisco apparently was. He figured that McBride fella would skip out as soon as may be. He knew he was smarter than Brisco thought. Of course Lem would never say that to Brisco. Why provoke a fight? He knew all along Brisco had underestimated the young trader. Lem hadn't. But then, that was one of Brisco's major faults: He thought his cleverness was unsurpassable.

"What if I don't wanna git up yet?" Farley mumbled. Brisco's 'hawk spun through the air and buried itself two inches deep in the log on which Farley rested his head.

Farley was awake now, his bleary eyes fixed in shock on the granite-faced man standing over him.

"You're a crazy man, Brisco!" Lem said. "You wanna kill him?"

"If I had wanted to kill him, he'd be dead. And you will be, Farley, unless you get the hell up!" Farley struggled with his blankets, rolling to his knees. Brisco reached in front of him and yanked his tomahawk from the log. Farley didn't relax until Brisco put it away.

"We're pulling out. Get your gear together."

Farley began putting his pack together as Lem, an older man in his forties, sprinkled dirt over the still burning embers of their campfire. Lem ventured, "Where's our man headed, Brisco?"

"Fort Pitt," he spat out.

"How did he slip past you, Brisco? I thought you was watchin' him?" Farley asked before Lem could signal him to be quiet. Brisco leveled his cold gaze at Farley like he was aiming a gun, fists clenched at his sides.

"Shut your filthy mouth or I'll shut it for you—permanently!"

Farley got to his feet pulling his pack on his back. "Brisco . . ."

Brisco spun around. "Now what?"

"We ridin' after him? Should I get the horses?"

"No. We go on foot."

"We'll move faster on horseback," Lem offered tentatively.

"Aw," Farley whined, "I thought we was gonna ride." Farley just didn't know when to keep his trap shut, Lem thought. He waited for Brisco to explode, but he didn't. He managed to rein in his temper. He explained the situation to Farley as if he was a dunce.

"It'll be better on foot. With all of this Indian trouble, horses will attract unwanted attention. Anyway, he'll hear us coming if we're riding. We can sneak up on him better if we're on foot."

Brisco was staring into space, seeing it all in his mind's eye. "With three heavily loaded packhorses, he'll be moving slowly himself. We should catch up with him quick. Once we put him out of business, we'll have his horses." His hand went to his 'hawk automatically.

Lem doubted it. He thought that McBride had a pretty good start on them. And as for sneaking up on him . . .

"Any more questions?" Brisco snapped at Farley, who was looking unhappy.

"No," Farley answered submissively.

As he got his gear together, Lem mused for the hundredth time how he ever picked up such a traveling partner. They were entirely different. And Lem was always pulling Farley's bacon out of the fire before it got singed. He was a big, stupid, lazy man—but he was Lem's partner. He was used to him now.

"I'll go pick up the Allyn kid."

"Who's he?" Lem asked curiously.

"Just some dumb kid I picked up. No need to know more."

Chapter Twelve

Molly made little progress the next day. So fearful was she of being set upon by savages that she proceeded at a pitifully slow pace. Each mile she traveled alone, her fears grew.

When the wagon wheel made an inordinately loud creak, she stopped to look it over for damage. She just couldn't afford to have the wagon disabled now. It turned out to be nothing but her nerves playing tricks on her. When a hidden branch cracked and crunched under the horses' feet, she was sure the sound carried for miles.

Having the entire burden lying constantly on her inexperienced shoulders wore her down. She had a fanciful idea that luck was running out on her, that it was only a matter of time before something terrible happened. By late afternoon, they had traveled only a few piddling miles. But at least they had not been discovered, she thought with weary triumph. For her, that was no small achievement.

Sliding off the horse, she almost tripped from exhaustion. Her back ached from sitting in the saddle all day. Her arms felt heavy as lead, as she once again broke off branches to cover what little of the wagon still showed where she had stopped it under some trees.

Afterward, Molly walked back down her trail and tried to eradicate all evidence of their passing. Although she had not seen signs of Indians, she did not relax.

While the horses were eating, Molly took stock of their supplies. Just enough to get them back to Bewilderness. If only she dared use her rifle, she might shoot some game. Molly was not a bad shot at all. But the rifle's report would bring down on them every warrior in the area. There was the sound of a stream nearby, but she didn't dare leave her father for the hour or so it might take to do some fishing. Instead, Molly carefully divided the food into small daily portions and gave her father his share.

Aaron Fletcher made himself swallow it although Molly could see he had no appetite. As Molly gave him the tea, she wondered solicitously if the little girl had ever been caught for taking it. The poor little mite!

Resolving to stand guard that night, Molly slumped down on her blankets and sat, eyes closed, for a few minutes. Just for a few minutes, she promised herself.

But her body slowly slipped sideways, then to the ground, and she immediately dropped off to sleep.

Molly slept long and deeply, waking with a start at daylight to the chatter of birds. Good heavens! She'd slept all night with no one to watch their camp! Scrambling out of her blankets, she went to her father. Even to her worried ears, his breathing seemed less labored. Folding up the blankets, Molly started collecting wood.

It was a beautiful morning. The sun was shining through the leaves and made pretty patterns on the grass. As Molly got a small fire going and hung an old pot filled with water over it, she noticed some squirrels sitting in a tree eating nuts. Suddenly, they dropped what they were eating and whisked up the tree. Then the birds flew into the sky.

At that same instant Molly heard a noise. Dropping the kindling to the ground soundlessly, she grabbed up her gun then disappeared into the trees. Someone was out there, she thought. Breathlessly, she ducked behind a bush. Molly could hear them moving around stealthily. *Indians?*

Her heart started pounding in her chest. Were there very many? Could she hold them off? How could she warn her father?

For a second she remained where she was, undecided, then Molly circled around to where the noise came from. Now she could see a dark shadow. She paused. It appeared to be only one man after all. Thank goodness! One, she might be able to handle. Somehow he had found their trail and was following it. People didn't track other people out here just from idle curiosity. He wanted something! She was sure of it!

Well, whatever he wanted, he wasn't going to get it! Her face set in hostile lines, and she went after him like a hunter. She sidled closer. He was bent down intently studying the trail. Vexation at his audacity warred with fear of his intent. He must have evil intentions, else why did he creep about?

Molly's mouth firmed for the unpleasant task ahead. She didn't relish shooting anyone, but she would if she had to. Slowly, silently, for she was a light girl, Molly moved up behind him. When she was near enough, she saw that it was a white man! What did he want? Why was he slinking around here?

Chapter Thirteen

Brisco made himself calm down when he went to fetch Ben. He didn't want him to sense that anything was wrong. He had a use for him.

"Allyn!" Brisco forced himself to keep a distance from the open-faced lean-to and call out, when everything inside of him wanted to kick the stuffing out of the boy and yell at him to hurry. Fortunately Ben, a light sleeper, awoke instantly. He got to his feet. Unlike Lem and Farley who took precious time to orient themselves, Ben was wide awake.

"Mr. Brisco?" He stood just inside the entry and peered out into the moonlight.

"Yes, it's me," he said, stifling the irritation in his voice. "Are you ready to leave right now? I've got Lem and Farley waiting for us down the road."

Ben was up, pulling on his moccasins, then reaching for his shirt. "Lem and Farley?"

"Two other men I got to help me. They're reliable," he lied. "I'll meet you down by the fork in the road in twenty minutes."

"I'll be there," Ben said, stuffing a few belongings into his pack. He had not expected to leave as soon as this, but Brisco disappeared before he could question him. Why did they have to light out in the middle of the night like this? Why didn't Brisco warn him they would be leaving soon? Even in the dark, Ben could tell by his voice that he was annoyed about something. Naturally, he didn't tell Ben anything. It seemed as if Brisco hadn't planned this very well at all.

Brisco strode back to the other camp. "Aren't you ready yet?" He watched angrily as Farley was still trying to pack his gear. "The longer you take, the farther McBride will have gone."

"Who?" Farley finally got it all into his pack and was fastening it clumsily.

"Rusty McBride, you nitwit."

Farley's eyes flickered with knowledge. "Trader? Sleepin' in Wilder's stables?"

"I tole ya," Lem said patiently.

"No ya never. Ya said it's not important."

"Well, what of it?" Lem asked, ready to leave.

"I was up at the tavern today. That McBride fella took off two days ago."

"What?" Brisco spat out. "What are you talking about? Are you sure? Why the hell didn't you tell me? Clod! We could have gotten him by now!"

"No one tells me nothin'," Farley whined. "If ya woulda, I coulda tole ya that that thar Andy Jackson run him outta town."

Brisco frowned. "Are you sure about that?"

"Sure I am. Jackson's friends all tole me how he called him a coward and a purty boy and he jest took it. Lifted up his petticoats and ran out to the stables scared as a jack rabbit. Jackson even offered to fight him alone, but he snuck outta town in the middle of the night because he was too afeared to meet him agin."

Brisco smiled. This put a new light on things. No wonder he had slipped through his hands. Come to think of it, it was more like "ran" through his hands. When McBride had shot him in the stable, his shot must have been sheer luck.

Interesting. So he's not the tough guy I thought he was. Even better. He had probably been scared off by him as well, Brisco thought scornfully. The two incidents had just been too much for McBride. He'd be even more cowardly if they met him by himself— without the interfering tavern keeper to help him!

Lem saw the smile and felt safe to comment, "Should be easy pickins."

Brisco continued to smile. "Easier than I thought." Then he added, looking at Farley's vacuous face, "One more thing. No need to tell this Allyn boy what's what.

Maybe we'll need him, maybe we won't. No use cutting him in if we don't have to." Lem smiled wryly. Yeah, that's what Brisco probably figured about them as well.

A little while later, Ben was at the fork in the road and was introduced to both Lem and Farley. They gave him a curt nod, but didn't speak.

"But why do we—"

Brisco cut him off abruptly. "No talking. Let's get going. Our man has two days' start on us." He turned on his heel and headed through the woods. Lem and Farley followed and Ben came last, swinging his pack across his broad shoulders.

Although he had only seen Brisco's companions for a few moments, Ben was not impressed with them. They were the kind of men he instinctively avoided. They had a furtive air about them and the fact that they lived outside the town made him uneasy. On the other hand, the looks they gave him were speculative, as if they were wondering about him as well. The tight little grin that Lem gave him didn't make Ben feel any better. It was almost amused—as if he knew something Ben didn't—which was hard to believe.

From his contemptuous treatment of him, Lem managed to make Ben feel young and naive, almost like a fool. Why should he think that? Ben wondered. He, at least, had a valid grudge against Minks. These two were merely going because they were being paid.

Ben tried to carry on a conversation with them, just to be polite, but Lem and Farley refused to participate outside of a few grunts and one-syllable words. Ben couldn't know that they were afraid to give away what they fancied was their secret. Ben shrugged. He didn't care. They were unpleasant anyway.

Brisco wasn't much better when it came to imparting even the smallest of facts.

He stood aloof, not seeming to enjoy the company he was in either, even though he had selected it himself. He was always in the lead, expecting everyone to keep up without displaying any concern if they did or not. Brisco sure was angry at Kenny Minks, Ben concluded. He could sympathize with this feeling—at first.

As they supposedly tracked Minks, Ben began to have second thoughts about joining forces with Brisco. He told himself he had no choice, however, because that no-good swindler, Kenny Minks, had stolen from him and he wanted revenge. Why shouldn't he? Ben's hands were still cut and raw from chipping out those two canoes he'd stolen. For the past few days, he had been digging splinters out of his hands and it was downright painful! He made himself a promise that if he ever got hold of Minks, he'd take him apart. He'd earned that money! He'd get it one way or another.

Ben studied the two men hired by Brisco with little enthusiasm. A more seedy, corrupt-looking pair of bounders he'd never seen before. Brisco was no judge of men. Normally, he would have nothing to do with men like these. He almost pitied Kenny Minks when they caught up with him—almost. But even though it would be four against one, you needed all the edge you could get when facing Minks. Besides, a thief like Minks shouldn't expect fair treatment. He had forfeited that right.

"Wagons!" Farley pointed out the ruts in the ground the next day.

"Train's goin' to Fort Pitt," Lem agreed. "Damn his hide, our man is followin' them. Hidin' his tracks in with theirs."

"He won't be following them for long," Brisco shrugged.

"Why not?" Ben asked.

"Indians." Brisco indicated the other prints of un-shod ponies churning up the wagon wheel tracks. "Probably catch up to them when they get far enough out then cut them up good." Brisco predicted this in such a cold, emotionless voice that Ben could only stare at him. The icy profile showed no compassion.

"Couldn't we warn them?" Ben asked, shocked.

Brisco slung around. "What for? You want to get hacked up too? I don't!" He sounded furious at the pre-posterous suggestion. Lem and Farley didn't look very concerned either. They nodded at Brisco's words.

"What da ya wanna git yerself mixed up in other people's business for?" Farley asked, puzzled. "They're headed fer trouble, why go down with 'em?" Brisco turned back and continued to lead the way.

Lem and Farley followed. Ben went as well, but wasn't ready to drop the subject. "But there are women and children there." Brisco turned around so fast, Lem and Farley ran into him. He gave them a push that sent Lem into Farley and Farley sprawling onto the ground.

"Listen boy! When you're with me, you do what I tell you! If those people are too stupid to watch out for themselves, they deserve to be killed! I don't intend to spend my time being shepherd to a lot of fools! They made their choice, now let them live with the consequences."

Ben thought about that for a good long while. More and more he asked himself if *he* had made the right choice. Back at Bewilderness, Brisco had seemed a sociable man who was concerned with Ben getting his money back. Now, after three days in the woods, he was completely different. Ben wondered if Brisco thought him a fool as well. Perhaps he was. What, after all, did he know of James Brisco? Farley and Lem, it was plain to see, were scavengers hired to do dirty work. Wasn't that a reflection on Brisco as well? Ben was to see for himself the true character of his comrades.

Like Rusty McBride, they soon came upon the massacre. The stench was noticeable from a mile back. Even so, Ben was not prepared for the awful sight. He could only stare as they came upon the open field of butchered bodies littering the ground.

They all stopped at the edge of the woods. After a quick look to see if any Indians were around, the other three moved forward. It took Ben longer to take it all in.

"Someone's been here and covered the bodies," he said, his gray eyes sliding away from a bundle not five feet away. Although they were covered, arms and legs still showed. Blood had soaked through the cloths.

"Probably that thar trader," Lem grunted, walking over to a wagon and looking in. He did not appear to mind the small, still form underneath. Ben felt like gagging.

"Kenny Minks? I can't imagine him covering up these bodies," Ben finally said.

"Hee haw!" Lem laughed at the thought. "I cain't neither. I meant McBride."

"McBride?" Ben said stupidly.

"The man with the silver. The one we're after," Lem said, temporarily forgetting Brisco's orders to keep silent. "Only he'd do a fool thing like this—covering up the dead with good blankets." He kicked the edge of one that was covering a body. "I could have got me two dollars for that one." Ben could only stare at him, uncomprehendingly.

"I thought we were following Kenny Minks."

Lem realized his mistake. "Damn it, I plumb fergot! Well, you might as well know now as later. We're after Rusty McBride. Got hisself a load of silver by tradin' with the Injuns. Figured to git it fer ourselves."

"You mean it doesn't belong to Brisco? He promised me a hundred dollars to help him get it back."

At that, Lem, who was rummaging through a trunk, began to laugh derisively. "Brisco? Tradin' with the

Injuns? Why, they hate the sight of him! And workin' for his money—that'll be the day. Lookee here, boy, you stay with us and we'll split the silver, but don't be askin' any questions where it come from, see? 'Cause it makes it look bad for us. Do you understand what I'm sayin'?" he asked, squinting at the boy.

"Oh yes," Ben said quietly. "I understand."

"Good. Then if yer a smart young pup, you'll git yerself some extry money by goin' through the wagons and pickin' up what ya can. If ya don't git nothin' don't expect us to share ours with ya." With that, Lem climbed into the wagon. Farley was already going through another wagon and yelled with delight when he found a small, flat, wooden box.

"Sure to be somethin' here," he said. Brisco elbowed his way over and grabbed the box. "Now lookee here, Brisco, I found it—"

"I'll take care of the loot and split it when I decide we'll split it—and that's when the job is done." He took the box and started to walk away with it.

"We want to see what's in it!" Lem shouted, climbing down from the wagon. Farley followed, closing in on Brisco.

Ben was watching it all with a horrified look on his young face. He began to back up slowly. They were not going after Brisco's property at all. These three men were criminals, prepared to kill an innocent man for his silver. Ben knew it was time to leave. As Brisco had said, a man had to live with his choice—and this was not his choice. When he backed to the edge of the woods, he turned around and melted silently away. He could still hear them quarreling as he started to run.

Brisco pried open the box. There were some coins and a few trinkets. There were also letters. Brisco took the letters and tossed them onto the ground. He pocketed the coins and jewelry.

"Well, go on," he snarled as they stood watching him. "Go look for more." After a long moment, Lem and Farley moved off.

"That was mine, Lem," Farley complained. "That belonged to me."

"Don't worry. We'll get it back. Thievin' skunk!" Lem muttered.

After a while, Brisco noticed that Ben was nowhere to be seen. "Where's that Allyn boy?" he asked angrily, jumping out of a wagon and carrying some knives he had found. He looked all around but didn't see him. Lem and Farley came up carrying other booty. His cold eyes lit on Farley. "What did you tell him?" he pressed him in a threatening voice.

"I didn't tell him nothin'," Farley whined, taking a step backwards.

"I think he has a delicate stomach," Lem interceded, although never intending to reveal that he was the cause of Ben running off. "Didn't seem to appreciate this great opportunity he has here of gettin' some extry money."

"Damn," Brisco swore. "I was going to have him go into McBride's camp to throw him off guard."

"I don't think he'd a done it," Lem said quickly, stuffing money into his pocket while Brisco was occupied. "Once he found out it wasn't Kenny Minks—"

"What do you know about Kenny Minks?" he shot out. Lem saw his mistake.

"Well I did mention—"

"I knew you two couldn't keep your big mouths shut!" He grabbed Lem by the throat and began to squeeze with his powerful right hand. His fingers bit into Lem's flesh as he struggled to breathe. With his other hand, Brisco reached for his 'hawk.

Farley looked alarmed. Lem and him had been friends for nigh on ten years. "Now jest a minute, here!" he began heatedly. "You need us, damnit! Now that that boy is gone you need us bad. You know that!"

His hand stopped reaching for his 'hawk. Much as Brisco would like to split Lem's cranium, he realized the truth of it. The long fingers which had been grappling at Lem's throat slowly relaxed. Lem, who had been clawing in vain at the iron grip, collapsed to the ground gasping for breath, his face purple. Farley clumsily patted him on the back thinking this would help.

"Now get going and look for more valuables, and remember, don't try hiding anything from me." He went back to the Millers' wagon where, unknown to Lem and Farley, he had found a pearl necklace hidden in a coffee pot.

"Ya all right, Lem?" Farley asked his friend who was on all fours, hacking and coughing, trying to suck air into his lungs. It was a long while before Lem could talk, then he whispered for some water. Farley got it for him.

"Son of a bitch!" he swore. He was barely able to swallow the water, his throat was so constricted. "I tell ya, Farley. I ain't never seen the likes of him. I bet he'd kill his own mother." He paused. "If he ain't already." Lem got up slowly. He touched the tender red welts on his throat, then flinched. "Let's git goin'," he said hoarsely. "I think I saw me some gold coins in that wagon."

Ben raced about a mile before he slowed down to a jog. His mind was still reeling when he thought of what he had narrowly escaped. If he hadn't been so furious, he would have seen through Brisco at once. He remembered his mother telling him one time, "When a stranger wants to do you a favor—watch out!"

Ben could imagine what would have happened to him later, when McBride was waylaid and killed. Brisco was very quick with his knife. Ben knew he would have no qualms about using it on him too. And he would have to, because once he found out their quarry was not Kenny Minks, there was no way in hell he'd have any part of the murder.

Ben stopped. Shouldn't he warn this Rusty McBride? In some way he felt responsible. Ben shook his head. It was no use. He'd never outstrip Brisco. He was like a bloodhound when it came to smelling out money. Ben was not the woodsman Brisco was. He could never track McBride in time. Moreover, the three of them would surely kill him if they thought he was going to interfere. Ben admitted to himself that he couldn't handle all three. Regretfully, the only thing he could do now was to go back to Bewilderness. He picked up his speed to a mile-eating pace.

Chapter Fourteen

The next day, Ben stopped to rest. He had spent a solitary night sleeping on the hard ground under some bushes. He had managed to put quite a distance between himself and his erstwhile companions. Not that he thought that Brisco and his cronies would come after him. Brisco was in too much of a hurry to rob that trader to waste his time. Ben smiled humorlessly when he realized how easily he'd been led along by James Brisco. Recovering his stolen silver! No wonder that Lem character had given him such a look. It had "fool" written all over it.

Ben shifted his pack to rest more easily on his back. Well, Lem and Farley were the fools now. Let them handle Brisco when the time came. Frankly, he didn't think they could do it. Underhanded as they were,

Brisco outstripped them when it came to stabbing others in the back. Literally and figuratively.

Indians again! About one hundred feet away a small war party snaked silently through the thick greenery. Ben ducked behind some bushes. As he did, his foot shot out from under him and he stumbled. Instinctively, he put out his hands and managed to drop silently to the ground, hugging it. The bushes hardly moved. As he peered through the foliage, he saw about twelve braves moving briskly, each carrying a rifle. As quickly as they came, they vanished into the shadows.

When he was sure they were gone, he got up rubbing his ankle. Looking down, Ben saw what had made him stumble. He frowned.

Wagon ruts!

These were visible to the naked eye for only a few feet. Someone had carefully covered them up, but he could see they were deep and recent. What was a lone wagon doing here in the middle of nowhere? Had someone survived the massacre? But no, that didn't make sense. The Indians had been thorough. He had witnessed exactly how thorough. No one could have gotten away, much less a whole wagon.

Ben continued to follow the signs left by the wagon. Someone had been meticulous enough to cover every indication of their passing. But there were always left behind bits and pieces to read. Ben had found a gash low down on a tree trunk from a hub scraping against it. He was surprised the wheel didn't break. The driver obviously didn't know what he was doing. A wad of black hair was caught on a thorn where a horse had been led. Broken pieces of twigs, the insides still green, indicated how recently they had been snapped.

Finally, Ben came upon some footprints. Two people. One a man, judging by the larger size, and the other was a child or girl. After a while, he saw only the child's prints. What had happened to the man?

Ben trailed them for miles before he realized they were looking for places to hide. They were not taking a direct route back to Bewilderness, but Ben knew that was the general direction they were headed. Their route was more circuitous. That meant for some reason they needed to fort up someplace along the way. They were smart enough not to stay at one place too long. Also, he frowned, they didn't seem to make much progress, covering only a few miles a day.

It was early morning of the next day when he finally came upon the wagon. It had been covered with bushes and deadfall, but whoever had done it had either been in a hurry or was not very proficient. Immediately, Ben saw the wilting leaves hanging from branches that had been broken off and put there at least twelve hours before. If any Indian came by he would notice it in an instant.

Ben moved up closer and saw the meager camp. No one was in sight. A small fire was burning with a pot suspended over it. He sniffed. Tea? He wrinkled his nose. It smelled something like it. He moved closer. No one seemed to be around. There was no movement from the wagon and the fire was unattended. How careless they were!

Behind him, the click of a rifle being cocked broke the stillness like a snapping twig. Ben stiffened.

"You'd better have a good reason for spying on us," a female voice said coolly. Ben relaxed. A girl, not a child. He put his arms up, still holding his rifle.

"Can I turn around?" he asked quietly.

"I expect," she said grudgingly. "But don't try anything or you're dead where you're standing!"

Ben turned and tried to hide his surprise. A lovely brown-eyed girl stood there, with blond curling hair smothered under an old hat. She stood tall and slim with her rifle aimed right at his midsection. His eyes lingered on the blond curls. A brave would love to have that hanging from his belt! It prodded him to speak urgently.

"What are you doing here, miss? Don't you know there are Indians around?"

"Of course I do! We've been dodging them for days!" Her pretty mouth tightened. "What business is it of yours?"

He looked at her, then at the wagon. Enlightenment dawned. "You're from the wagon train, aren't you? The one that's up ahead?"

She lifted her chin a fraction of an inch almost haughtily, not liking to be reminded of it, especially by a stranger. "What of it? You weren't part of it," she replied shortly, not meeting his eyes. "I suppose they told you about us? Well, I don't care! The Millers had no right to do what they did!"

"I don't know what you're talking about," he said bluntly. "Me and my . . . acquaintances . . . were trailing it. Did you know it was attacked by Indians?"

She paled. Her rifle lowered a fraction then she determinedly lifted it up again. In disbelief she swallowed hard and asked, "Are they all right? Were there many injured? Do they need help? We don't have much, but—"

"They were all killed."

"That's impossible," she said, trying to grasp the enormity of it. He could see that she was shocked. People grew mighty close when they traveled together. Neighbor always helped neighbor. "There were so many people," Molly whispered.

"Yes, but no one kept a guard, and I found signs of rifles leaned against trees instead of in men's hands where they belonged. Whoever ran it didn't know what they were doing." His shortness was for waste of life that shouldn't have been.

"Some of the men tried to tell the Millers but they never listened. But are you sure they're all dead?" she asked, ashen-faced. "I knew all of those people. Most of them were good, kind folks."

"All dead," he told her gently but firmly. "I can testify to that. And you'll be dead, too, if you don't get a move on."

She bit her lip and glanced indecisively towards the

wagon. After all, what did she know about him? He sounded genuine, yet you never knew. She came to a decision. "Thank you for the warning, mister. We'll be fine."

She did not, however, lower her rifle, Ben noticed. He couldn't understand her stubbornness in the face of what he had just told her. Ben looked again at the empty camp. "Are you alone?" he ventured.

Immediately she was suspicious. "Certainly not!"

He sighed. "I only ask because you can't drive that wagon yourself. I can help you if you let me."

"Why should I trust you? Why do you want to help me?"

"Maybe because I don't want to see your pretty hair hanging from a buck's war belt." He said it deliberately and saw her horrified face. "I almost ran into a war party yesterday. Only a matter of time before they find you."

"Molly." A weak, but definitely male voice called from the wagon. Molly stood there debating what to do. She wanted to see her father but she didn't want to take her rifle off the stranger. "Molly," it came again.

"I'll go." Ben deliberately turned his back on her and made for the wagon. He did not bother to see if she was following.

"Wait a minute!"

Ben paid her no heed, but he strode purposefully over to the back of the wagon where the voice seemed to be coming from. Molly, half exasperated, half admiring his boldness, hurried after, the rifle in her hand no longer pointing at him but at the ground.

"Good morning, sir, my name is Ben Allyn," Ben said as Mr. Fletcher pulled aside the canvas flaps. Ben saw a man in his early forties who was struggling into a sitting position. He seemed to be the only occupant of the wagon. Sweating profusely, Aaron managed to pull himself up.

"Hello," he said in a strong voice even though he looked about done in. "I'm Aaron Fletcher and this here is my daughter, Molly. What seems to be the trouble?"

Ben explained about the wagon train and the fate of the people. He warned him about the war party nearby and how dangerous their position was. He carefully avoided talking about himself or what he was doing in the woods alone. Aaron Fletcher didn't ask. Instead, Ben could feel those keen eyes studying him closely. Ben flushed a little. He had nothing but his pack and rifle. He couldn't blame the man for being wary. He would, too, if he had a pretty daughter. Ben saw Aaron smile ruefully and ease back. Maybe he saw something in Ben that reassured him. He hoped so.

Aaron nodded sadly at the death of his friends. "Them Millers never knew what they were doin'. Never took advice from anyone. Pity everyone had to suffer from their stupidity." He was silent a moment. "So you tracked us, did you?"

"Yes, sir. And if I can track you," he said earnestly, "the Indians sure can. Because," he explained honestly, "I'm no tracker."

Aaron smiled a little at that. "I was worried we were leaving our mark. Hard to hide a wagon like this."

"If you let me help you," he began almost shyly, "I can drive the wagon. We can go back the way I came. It'll be shorter and the Indians might not expect that."

Aaron considered him for a long moment. He saw character in the young man's face. Strength and pride too. At last he said, "Thank you, Mr. Allyn. I'd be grateful for your help. I've been that worried about Molly." He gave him a quick grin.

Ben seemed pleased. "I'll get the horses. There's no time to lose."

When he was out of hearing, Molly turned to her father and asked, "Are you sure you can trust him, Pa?"

"If he'd been up to no good, he wouldn't have offered to help us, especially when he found there's just two of us. He could have killed us both at any time. Besides," he sighed, "we ain't got anything he would want." He patted her hand. "'Cept you." Then he added, "Good-looking young man."

"Pa!"

"Well, he is. Got a right to my opinion, ain't I? Seems honest, too, and looks you straight in the eye. I've always liked a man who can look you in the eye."

"I'd better go help him." Taking her rifle, she trudged to where he was hitching up the team. As she stopped to watch him, she noticed his light brown hair, cut short so that it curled at his collar. Pa was right. She liked his direct gray gaze and firm chin. Still, she'd hold off giving her opinion yet. Time would tell. Molly guessed him to be a few years older than she.

"It's nice of you to help us," she said stiffly, "though I don't know why you're doing it."

He smiled as he worked on the horse but he did not look up at her. "You're a suspicious little thing."

"A girl has to be."

His mouth slanted down at the corners. "You're right. A little suspicion can save you a lot of grief later," he said grimly. "Hadn't you better see to the fire?"

"Oh, yes!" Molly had forgotten and rushed over to take the pot down. Afterwards, she sprinkled dirt to douse the flames.

Before putting the lukewarm pot of water back in the wagon, she poured her father a cup of tea. "Here, take it, Pa. It's only warm but it will do you good." He looked at it with disfavor.

"I think you should have some too."

"I'm not sick."

"You will be if you drink this," he said, shuddering as he sipped it. Molly smiled, glad to see he was feeling a little better. Good enough to joke, anyway. She politely asked Ben if he would like a cup of tea before they left.

His mouth tugged to one side in a smile. "No thanks, I just heard your father's opinion of it." She pursed her lips, a little offended, then turned away and started to giggle. Ben grinned as she climbed into the wagon.

Chapter Fifteen

With Ben Allyn taking charge—and he did take charge, Molly noticed—they made much better time. They covered in one day what it took Molly to do in two. He was always giving orders and checking to see that they were carried out correctly. If he wasn't so welcome, she would have become very annoyed with him. It was nice, however, to have a man in charge again. Already, she felt more easy knowing that the responsibility was lifted from her shoulders and put onto Ben's sturdy ones. Unlike her father, who was slow to make his decisions and carefully considered all angles, Ben just naturally did what was best. He didn't, she noticed with some amusement, consult her or her father.

"Maybe we should camp here," she suggested that afternoon as they came to a nice-sized thicket.

"No." Ben shook his head decisively. "There's a place farther on that I've been thinking of."

"You know best," she said ironically.

"Thank you, I think I do." They looked at each other and then began to smile.

"Did anyone ever tell you that you're too modest?"

"Nope! No one ever did," he answered cheerfully. "The hollow should be right past these pines." It was, and Molly had to admit that it was a good place to stay. The hollow was well-hidden and shallow, and a fast-moving freshet ran through it.

"It is good," she admitted.

"That wasn't hard, was it?" he asked, patting the horses after they had stopped. "To admit that I was right?"

"I wouldn't mind admitting it if you weren't so darned pleased with yourself," she returned, helping him with the horses.

"You take a rest. I'll do that."

Molly blushed at his solicitude then went to check on her father. While she described to him the place where they had camped, she watched Ben unhitch the horses. He spoke gently to them then led them to water. Her father was right. He was nice.

Aaron Fletcher noticed that Molly kept her eyes on young Allyn even as she spoke to her dear ol' pa. He smothered a smile. His little Molly was definitely interested in the young man. He was relieved. Bringing up a daughter without a wife was hard enough but getting her married to a nice man was worse. He'd have to encourage Allyn to stick around. Molly would like that and so would he.

"Think I'll get up tonight, Molly. I'm getting cramped sittin' in one spot all day." He began to rise. Immediately, Ben was there helping him. Aaron eased himself down on a big log and watched as the two young people settled in for the night.

Ben collected wood and hauled water to the cook fire. When he put the wooden buckets down, flecks of blood appeared on his hands.

"Your hands!" Molly exclaimed with concern. He reddened and tried to hide them. But she insisted on seeing them and he finally showed them to her. There were still plenty of splinters visible.

"Splinters! Look, Pa! Look at Ben's hands. How painful that must be!"

"I was making some canoes," he explained to Mr. Fletcher, embarrassed about the fuss she was making. It had been a long time since anyone had made a fuss over him. Never had a girl done it—especially not a pretty one.

"I'll get my needle and pick them out for you," Molly said, and was as good as her word. Ben sat there obediently as Molly took his hand in both of hers. Mr. Fletcher tried not to smile when Molly laid it on her lap and began to gently pick out the slivers. Their heads were close together and Ben was pleasantly aware of her nearness. It showed on his face.

"Just yank them out," he said in a manly voice, yet liking the feel of her small, graceful hands on his far too much. From this close he could see her dark feathery lashes laying against her soft cheeks. Her hair smelled like soap. Ben liked it very much. Just then, she looked up straight at him with her big brown eyes and he gave her a sappy smile. She seemed to like it because she applied herself even more happily to her task, scooting over a little closer to him. To see better, she explained.

"There," she said when she had gotten out every one. "That's done. Now I'll just wash them with warm water." Molly bustled over to the fire where some water was almost boiling, and used some to wash away the blood. "I have a piece of cotton somewhere to wrap on your hands—"

"No need," Ben said quickly, shoving his hands in his pockets. "They'll heal better in the open air. I'm much obliged to you, though."

"That's quite all right. It's the least I can do for helping us this way." Aaron's lips twitched at her adult voice. Yep, Molly was definitely interested. After that, the girl swished around getting dinner ready. As she did it, she sent many an appreciative look in Ben's direction as he worked.

His eyes were definitely gray, Molly decided, a color she personally liked very much. His hair, though brown, had a blond gleam in it. Stirring the pot dreamily, she thought of the other boys who had courted her.

Some of them were nice but none as good-looking as Ben. Even Douglas Benson, who had begged her to marry him two years ago at a tender sixteen, faded in comparison to Ben Allyn. She had to admit, she couldn't see Douglas leading them through Indian territory as swiftly and as surely as Ben was doing. Although he was a bit overconfident, she found that this was not unattractive.

At dinner, Ben told them about Kenny Minks and how he had run out without paying him for his work. He did not mention Brisco or the other men. He allowed the Fletchers to think he had come this way for the sole purpose of looking for Minks.

"You mean he didn't pay you?" Molly was fired up, all set to defend Ben. "What are you going to do?"

"He'll turn up again," Aaron said slowly. "He's like a bad penny." Then he paused. "But you go slowly with him, son. Don't be goin' at him hotheaded. No one will blame you for gettin' your money from him, but you go for anything more and you'll be the one in the wrong."

It was as if, Ben thought ashamed, Aaron could read his mind. "I can't deny my first thought was to find him and lick the tar out of him," he admitted. "But I've changed my mind since then." Unconsciously, his eyes flicked to Molly where she sat watching him, wide-eyed and sympathetic. Somehow he didn't think she'd be so sympathetic if he beat Kenny Minks to within an inch of his life.

"Smart thing," Aaron interrupted his thoughts. "You

don't want to become known as a man who can't hold on to his temper. Anyone can lose it, but only a few smart ones can keep it."

"Like money," Molly giggled. "Does anyone want some more corn bread?" To her delight, her father asked for a bit more.

"That restorative tea must be doin' the trick," he said. Nevertheless, he retired early, vowing that he'd be up and helping some tomorrow.

"No, you won't," Molly decreed as she saw her father to his bed. "Ben can handle it so just you don't worry."

"He's a good worker," Aaron admitted easily. "And he has honest brown eyes."

"Pa, they're gray," she exclaimed then, as her father chuckled, she blushed. She rushed to add, "I just happened to notice."

"I know. Just like you noticed he has blond hair!"

But Molly refused to rise to the bait and agreed that he had nice blond hair. "For a brunet," she added before bidding him good night.

Ben was watering the horses once more before turning in. Then he brought them a few wild apples he had picked up from the ground. "Treat your horses good and they'll do anything for you," he explained quickly.

"You don't have to excuse yourself for liking horses," Molly said. She had noticed how he patted them all the time. "That one is Merry. We bought her from a farmer on our way here." Molly reached out and stroked her mane. Accidentally, she brushed Ben's hand and they both yanked their hands away as if stung. "She—she's nice and steady," Molly said hurriedly. "Merry is my favorite. Do you have any horses?"

"Yes, Joe Wilder is looking after mine for me back at Bewilderness." He moved away. "You'd better get to bed. It's getting dark. I'll stand guard."

"I'll stand guard with you."

"You don't have to."

"I can't sleep anyway. I'll get some blankets." When Molly returned they both wrapped the blankets about them and sat side by side against a tree.

"What made you folks leave the wagon train?" Ben ventured after a long, companionable silence. "Didn't you want to go to Fort Pitt?"

"We did want to go but they threw us out because Pa was sick." At Ben's shocked and outraged expression, which was balm to her soul, she added, "Oh, not the other families. They were real nice to us. They didn't mind helping us along. But the Millers, a husband and wife, they threw us out. They organized the train, so it seems they had the right. Anyway, we couldn't have kept up."

Ben thought back to the massacre. "The Millers won't be bothering anyone now."

"I wouldn't wish that on them," Molly said, "even though they were so mean and spiteful. A lot of good folks died." She thought of the Kern family. "They all had such high hopes."

"At least you're alive. The Millers did you a good turn without knowing it." There was a long pause. "What will you and your father do now?"

Molly turned to him and confessed, "I didn't want to go to Fort Pitt. Everyone is going there. I saw this pretty valley near Bewilderness. It had good, sweet water and the ground was nice and flat. There were fields of wildflowers—"

"And a stand of black walnut trees around the south side of the clearing? On Saylor Creek?" Ben put in, hearing her describe the very place to which he had taken such a fancy.

She leaned away from him a little. "That's the one! Did you see it? Isn't it perfect?"

"It was nice," he said slowly. "Reminded me of my home when my ma was alive. I was thinking of building a cabin in that very same valley. Maybe start farming. I'd sure admire having some fruit trees too."

Molly saw his handsome face light up at the thought. "Maybe we could both—I mean, and Pa too—all three of us get a cabin built by winter then we could farm it together. It would be easier if we helped each other," she said warming to the idea. "And if you wanted, we could build a second cabin next year. In case you get tired of our company." Better leave him a way out, she told herself.

Ben thought about it and liked it, but all he said was "We'll see." Molly smiled in the dark. She couldn't see his face, which was probably annoyingly expressionless, but she could hear the note of possibility in his voice. He was considering the idea seriously. Molly had not been raised by a father without learning something about men. Now was not the time to press him. Men took an awfully long time to come to some decisions. She would just let it simmer in his mind awhile.

Contentedly, Molly relaxed and closed her eyes. Twenty minutes later she was asleep, her cheek resting against Ben's buckskin-clad shoulder. He could hear her light, steady breathing. To make sure she didn't slip sideways he put his arm around her, clasping her trim waist. He smiled into the darkness. It was very cozy. Then he moved a little closer.

The next day at breakfast Ben mentioned the valley to Mr. Fletcher while Molly dried the dishes.

"Mol took a fancy to it," Aaron admitted. "I wisht now I'd listened to her. Saved us a lot of time and bother."

"Maybe we could claim the land together," Ben suggested, trying to sound casual. "Become partners in the farm." Aaron wasn't fooled in the least by Ben's offhanded manner. The young man was serious about this and about Molly too. His eyes brightened up.

"That's a good idea! Think we could get the cabin done afore the snow sets in?"

"I'm sure of it," Ben assured him encouragingly. The thought of sharing a cabin and farm with father and daughter was vastly appealing. It was like having a family again. At twenty, Ben sorely missed it.

Aaron looked at the young man's face as if he sensed his loneliness. Like a lot of young men out here, he must have been on his own at an early age. But all Aaron said was, "And don't you be thinkin' I'm useless! When I throw this fever, watch out! I'll be able to keep up with you, and then some!"

Ben smiled. "I'll bet you will. So, should we head towards that valley?"

"No use wastin' time," Aaron agreed. "I'll help you with the horses." Aaron did, but he still tired easily and Ben tactfully recommended that he rest in the wagon.

"You'll need all your strength for cutting those logs," he said cheerfully. Aaron, knowing he was right, gave in. He didn't intend on young Allyn to do all of the work. At forty-two, he was still a powerful worker when he wasn't laid low by fever. He didn't want Ben to think he was getting a lame dog to care for.

"Well, Molly, are you ready to tackle that dream of yours?" Aaron asked. Molly's pretty face glowed. A heady feeling filled Ben and he could stare at her for only a few seconds. He didn't think she could get much prettier but he was wrong.

With a small smile on her face, Molly followed the wagon as Ben led them. From this angle she could admire his straight back, his broad shoulders and his confident posture. *Mrs. Molly Allyn,* she thought to herself. It sounded just right.

Chapter Sixteen

Rusty made good time the next day, stopping long enough only to rest the horses and have a cold meal. Isabelle ate everything enthusiastically, hot or cold. He hoped her aunt and uncle were good providers.

With great care, he made sure his trail twisted and wound about, taking advantage of dusty places that left no sign. Twice he crossed and recrossed the river, coming out on shields of rock. All the time he kept looking back and around him. Nothing disturbed the silence of the forest.

"Do you think we lost them varmints, Rusty?" Isabelle asked as he made dinner that evening.

"I don't know, but I doubt it."

Isabelle didn't complain at all. She was a good little girl and always wanting to help. It was as if she had to justify the food she ate. As a matter of fact, he enjoyed having her along. He hadn't realized how lonesome it was making a trip with just his horses to talk to. It was especially so at night when you wanted to relax and talk a bit. It was real nice the way Isabelle listened attentively to everything he said. Even if she didn't understand the half of it, she'd just nod her bright head and watch him closely.

That evening, he chose a small clearing just big enough for them and their animals in which to make camp. The fire couldn't be seen until you came within a few yards of it.

As Rusty got the fire going that evening, he came to a decision. He was getting plenty tired of packing up Isabelle and his horses every morning and making a run for it. It was time for some action. As he fed the fire, he came up with a plan. No need to tell Isabelle. It would only worry her. When it got dark and she was asleep, he'd do himself some hunting. Immediately, he felt better. It was time to take the fight to them. That was something they wouldn't expect.

"Want me to watch that bacon, Rusty?" Isabelle interrupted as she stared avidly at the bacon sizzling in the pan. "I'm real good at watchin' bacon."

Rusty tried not to smile. He knew that if Isabelle watched the bacon, there would be none left for dinner. "Thanks, Little Bit, but why don't you keep an eye on those beans? Beans need watching too."

Her face fell. "All right, Rusty. But I'm much better at watchin' bacon."

"It's a risk I'll take," he said gravely. She kept throwing so many longing looks at the thick slices in the pan that he got up for a moment and went to his pack.

"Here, Little Bit." He handed her a small package. "It'll make watching the beans easier," he said as she stopped stirring and opened it up.

"Candy!" she exclaimed in awe. "For me? All of it?" She looked at his face. He smiled and nodded. Quickly, she took them out and counted them. He need not have worried that she would eat them all up at once and become sick.

"I'll just have two a day," she announced. "That way they'll last longer. Did you want one, Rusty?" she offered shyly.

"No, I don't care for candy right now."

"I always do," she said, popping one into her mouth and enjoying it with considerable relish. She didn't mind watching the beans then. She stirred them so vigorously, Rusty had to tell her to stop.

Afterwards, she told him a little more about her rich upbringing. She also enumerated all of the fine things her family used to own. When she was finished, she yawned and admitted to being tired. Rusty covered her up, then he waited until he heard her deep breathing. She was fast asleep. Quickly, he moved. With good luck, she'd be out for the night. Gently picking up his rifle, he headed for the woods. He jumped, exasperated, at a voice behind him.

"Where are you going? You're not leaving me, are you?" Isabelle was sitting up and staring at him, scared.

He went over to her and put a reassuring hand on her shoulder. She was trembling. She must be scared of being left alone on her own for the third time: First her parents died, then the wagon train was attacked, now he was going.

"I'm just going out hunting, Little Bit," he said gently, softly. "You just stay here."

"Are you going to hunt Indians?" she asked, a little calmer.

"Nope. Wolves." He smiled.

"Wolves? Are they around?" A puzzled frown was on her smooth forehead.

"Yep. Whenever there's silver, the wolves will be there. The two-legged kind."

"You mean the varmints? Thieves?" she asked wisely.

"That's right. I'm going to scout around and see how many varmints we've got back there."

"Can I go with you?" Interest replaced her fear.

"No," he replied in a voice that brooked no arguing. "You stay here and watch things. If you hear anything, you get yourself behind that tree there. See? With the rocks around it? And stay put until I come back." She nodded. Smart as paint, she was.

"What if you don't come back?" She seemed almost afraid to ask.

"Don't you worry, Little Bit, I'll be back." His voice was grim. "No one's going to get me or my silver—or you," he added with a smile.

She appreciated being included. It seemed to make them inseparable. She nodded more happily.

"It may take me some time for I've got to move quietly and, if I find them, I'll want to listen in to what they're saying. All right?"

"It's all right with me, Rusty. As long as you're careful."

"I'm always careful. Now you be good." He patted her head awkwardly. Standing up, he moved towards the woods and vanished. Only the leaves, shaking slightly, were an indication that he had passed there.

Earlier that evening as Rusty made camp, he had noticed a faint light about a mile away. He figured on creeping up to the camp. It could be Brisco. He had to make sure.

When he got there, he saw only two men and neither one was James Brisco. One man was big with black eyes and black hair, his face covered with a growth of beard. The other was an older, weather-beaten man of about forty, lank, with graying hair and faded blue eyes. Both looked to be down-at-heel riffraff, the kind that hangs around the settlements looking for trouble. As he inched closer, he realized, with a start, that they were talking about him.

"Why ain't we come on him yet?" the big man was

grumbling as he drank his coffee. "Maybe we lost McBride."

"How could we? He's a goin' to Fort Pitt and this here is the way."

"Why ain't we come on any tracks yet, huh? Maybe he knows we're after him."

"He don't know nothin'!" the gray-haired man reacted strongly. "We're behind him. He cain't see our tracks."

"Yeah, well, we cain't see his neither. I say he's onto us or he's skedaddled somewheres else. Maybe to another settlement. Could be tryin' to outsmart us!" This thought had occurred to the lanky man and it annoyed him to have his suspicions confirmed by his dull-witted companion.

"Now lookee here, Farley. Two days ago he come across that massacre. You know it and I know it. Who else'd cover them bodies? So he's nearby and a headin' to Fort Pitt by the looks of it." Triumphantly he displayed his logic to his thick-headed friend.

Farley—the big, burly man—leaned forward. "But maybe he's changed his mind since then, Lem. Maybe he's seen them bodies and it starts him a thinkin'. And maybe he's a thinkin' he don't want to meet up with no Injuns. Them red devils sure cut them settlers down!" He paled at the thought. "What if he went back? What if he—"

"He didn't go back," a hard voice cut in from the far side of the camp. The two men jumped with surprise.

Rusty had seen what the two others hadn't: James Brisco had come from the woods on his left side. He was carrying a rifle and two dead rabbits. "Fine lookouts you are! McBride could come right up to you and you wouldn't even hear him!" His eyes narrowed with displeasure. "He's up ahead about a mile!"

Rusty's nerves tightened at this information. So he'd seen them, had he? Damnation! Rusty frowned worriedly.

"Skin these rabbits," Brisco ordered the burly man. It said much about Brisco that Farley, the larger man, readily obeyed.

"You found him? Let's git him!" Lem picked up his rifle. Rusty's hand started to lift his own. If they wanted to start anything, it would begin and end right here. Brisco would get the first bullet.

"Sit down!" Brisco's voice was sharp. Rusty eased his finger off the trigger. The other man sat. "We're not going yet. We know where they are and we have them where we want them. We'll go just before daybreak. He'll be asleep and they won't know what hit them." He smiled at the thought. He would do it in such an underhanded way, Rusty thought.

"Them?" Farley swung around. "You mean him?"

"I mean them," Brisco said shortly.

"He picked up some friends?" The lanky man didn't like it. "I knew it! I knew it would be too easy! Three to one is good odds, but if McBride's not alone, that changes things. I didn't count on more than one." Lem seemed to have become annoyed at the dark, grim man. "Or were you wrong, and there were more all along?"

Didn't Lem realize, even in his short acquaintance, that Brisco hated to be criticized? Rusty waited for the reaction.

"I wasn't wrong." Brisco's voice was low, deadly. "I'm never wrong. One man left the settlement. Are you calling me a liar?" Farley hastily turned to his rabbits. This was no fight of his.

Lem seemed to realize his mistake. Tension gripped him. Rusty knew what was going on in his head: Could he take Brisco? Brisco's black eyes glittered with hope. Wisely, Lem backed down. Brisco was too ready. If there had been a fight one of them would have ended up dead. Probably Lem. Still, it would have been one less with which to deal.

"'Course not," he muttered. The angry color left Brisco's face. "Well, if there was only him, where'd the others come from?"

"Escaped from the massacre." Brisco's good humor partially returned and he smiled.

"How many more?"

"One."

"We can take 'em on," Farley said.

Brisco gave a sharp laugh. "I'll say we can. The survivor is a little kid, about six years old."

"A little kid?" Farley asked. He and Lem both frowned.

"Little girl," he tossed off carelessly.

Farley put the rabbits down. "What are we gonna do? We can kill him, but not a girl. And if we let her go, she'll probably talk. I know she would. Little girls talk somethin' awful."

"Not with her throat cut, she won't," Brisco commented coolly.

The other two looked at each other. "Kill a kid? A little girl?" Farley looked worried. "I never kilt a kid before and if we get caught, sure enough we'll get strung up! Not even a trial!"

"I'll do it." He shrugged. "It'll be a pleasure." It sounded as if Brisco meant it.

"Even if you did"—Farley swallowed hard—"I mean, I don't mind killin' a man much. Anyway, someone totin' that much silver is jest naturally invitin' death, but a kid? If they find her, they'll know—"

"We'll scalp her," he said calmly. "Him too. After the massacre, they'll think it was the Indians. We'll dump them in the river." His voice was indifferent. "It'll be easy. I've scalped before. I've made lots of spending money taking in scalps to the Army."

Brisco didn't see the two men exchange looks.

"I don't mind floutin' the law now and agin," Lem admitted. "But I never scalped no one afore. Don't seem necessary, somehow. Once a person's dead that's the end of it." Farley nodded his agreement.

Brisco's unfriendly eyes flickered over them. "If you haven't got the stomach for it, then stay out of my way when the time comes." Brisco sank into silence, jabbing at the fire with a stick as if it was personal. The other two men avoided him, getting the meal ready.

As he sat there, Brisco dwelled pleasurably on what would occur on the morrow. Ever since he'd spotted the young trader's cache of silver, he knew he had to possess it. Aside from this, there was now another reason to rob McBride. Brisco hadn't forgotten how he had gulled him with those bags of dirt! His mouth clamped shut in anger as he thought of how McBride must have laughed as he hid them in the stables. And those little pups! He'd like to split open their skulls! Especially that Lonny! Calling him names! Automatically, his hand flicked down to touch his tomahawk as if unable to resist caressing the sharply honed edge. He was not through with any of them yet! First McBride, then the girl. If he had time he might make a quick stop at Bewilderness to give those whelps a comeuppance! He was breathing heavily as he quivered with anger.

He should have gone back and finished those boys off that night. That would teach McBride to send kids to do a man's work. He relaxed. Why worry? McBride wouldn't be around much longer himself. He would get him tomorrow—only a few hours more! Brisco looked forward to that more than getting the silver at this point. He had enjoyed tracking him and finding their campsite. He had seen how affectionate the trader was with the little girl. He actually liked her! All the better. Let him watch while he killed her. Brisco's lips turned up in a horrible smile. That's what he reveled in: stalking his prey, closing in on them, the hand-to-hand combat. He liked to watch their eyes when the hunted finally realized they were going to die. There was always a satisfying expression of fear in them before the final kill. Yes, tomorrow would be a real pleasure.

How would McBride react when they burst into his camp in the early hours? He would leave the trader to Farley and Lem. He'd go for the little girl. Maybe he'd just cut her throat right away. That would put McBride off his stride. After that, he'd be an easy target. Brisco enjoyed these thoughts for a few more moments, still stroking the blade of his 'hawk affectionately.

At last he got up to forage for more kindling. The other two men breathed a sigh of relief. Neither of them saw him halt just ouside the light of the fire and hunker down to watch his companions in the dark. They now spoke freely.

"Did ya see him, Lem?" Farley hissed. "Danged if he weren't feelin' for that hatchet of his again! He's always doin' it. Makes me feel real uneasy like." The sound carried clearly in the night air. It was quite loud enough for Brisco, only a few yards away, to hear.

"I know," Lem said sourly.

"I tell ya what! He's plumb crazy and that's the truth! Never shoulda joined up with him. If he's willin' to kill a kid, what about us? He looks like he cain't wait to use it!"

"Don't worry, Farley, soon as we get McBride and the

silver, we'll get rid of Brisco. I ain't gonna walk around waitin' for him to come up behind me in the dark!"

Farley was relieved that his friend had planned it out already. "Yeah, I sure don't like that look in his eyes. Reminds me of a rabidty wolf."

Neither one of them saw the ugly look that came over Brisco's face as he heard his partners plotting to get rid of him. If they had, they would not have been so indiscreet.

"Tomorrow," Lem went on, pouring himself more coffee, "we'll take care of Brisco—after we get the silver. Just stay near me and keep outta range of that 'hawk of his!"

"Think ya can take him, Lem?" Farley asked worriedly. "'Cause I don't think I can."

"I'll take him. Afore he takes us!"

Rusty had seen enough. He waited until Brisco finally loped off safely in the opposite direction. Then, taking advantage of the small sounds of activity, he slipped away quietly through the woods.

So, Brisco had seen their camp, had he? He knew about Isabelle so he probably was aware that she was his vulnerable spot! Damn his black soul to perdition!

Fortunately, he was now in possession of some very valuable information. While he had been watching the men he had formulated his plan. It was very simple: When Brisco came calling, he wouldn't find them at home. They would have to leave immediately, of course. There was no time to lose. Even now, Brisco might be too impatient to wait until morning. Even now he could be making his way back to Rusty's camp to try his luck. The thought made Rusty move more quickly.

Rusty caught his breath and slowed down when he came near his camp. Everything seemed to be quiet. He stopped and looked around slowly, searching the bushes and trees for any unfriendly presence. Nothing. He stepped into the clearing.

"Isabelle?" he called out softly. There was no reply. The girl's blanket was empty. Rusty's stomach lurched. Had Brisco come back? Had he gotten to her first? "Isabelle!" he called out a little more loudly.

"Here I am." The sound made him spin around. Isabelle, unhurt, was climbing out from behind the old tree. "Don't you remember, Rusty? You told me to hide here if anyone came. But I thought I'd get an early start." She was clinging to her moccasins. Rusty bent down and hugged her tightly, overwhelmingly relieved.

"I did forget," he admitted. "That was a good idea." He had only known the little scrap for a few days, yet he had never felt so glad to see anyone in his life. "You get yourself dressed, Isabelle. Time to be moving out."

"Did you find the varmints?" she asked, not even questioning his orders. Perhaps she heard the underlying urgency in his voice.

"Sure did. Three of them. They know we're here, so we have to be very quiet. All right? Their camp isn't far away."

"I'll get dressed," she promised in a whisper and grabbed her things. By the time he had packed and stoked up the fire, she was ready to go.

Rusty kept them going all night long and part of the next day before he called a stop. Knowing how close Brisco was, he had to be more watchful than ever. He also took fewer rests, even though the horses needed it.

Brisco would be hard to stop now. Once they broke into his camp and found only smoldering coals and his quarry long gone, his fury would know no bounds. He'd be after them in a minute. Unluckily for Rusty, Brisco was not hampered by packhorses and a small child, so he could move swiftly. It wasn't that Little Bit slowed him down, not in the least. She was anxious to please him and was quiet and obedient. Still, she was vulnerable. Damn! If only there was a place he could drop her off and continue on his own. If he was alone he could meet Brisco and his friends without worrying about what they would do to Little Bit.

That gave him an idea. He knew he couldn't outrun them forever. On the other hand, he couldn't take on all three of them at once unless he had plenty of luck—and Rusty never counted on that. But there was a way he could do it and have a chance to come out of it alive. He had to eliminate some of the players in this game. To do that, he would have to leave Isabelle by herself for a while. He didn't like the idea, but at this point he was out of aces. He had to do the unexpected before Brisco

even had time to think. Brisco liked planning ahead. He
didn't like surprises. That was why Rusty intended to
give him one.

Stopping the horses, Rusty lifted Isabelle down. "Isabelle, I've got to even the odds." She looked at him
questioningly. "I have a job for you to do. An important
one." His eyes were very serious. "I hope you can do it."

"I'll do anything you want, Rusty."

He knelt down in front of her and put a big hand on
each of her small shoulders.

"I have to go back and get those men on our tail.
While I'm gone, I want you to lead the animals along
slowly. Hopefully, those men will think I'm with you.
Keep on going towards those hills there." He pointed
ahead where they rose up above the treetops about two
miles away. "You'll come to a boulder field. You just
slow up there and wait. If you hear anything or see anyone, hide. And don't come out no matter what. If I
don't come back . . ." She shook a little. "I will come
back, but just in case I don't, you keep following the
trail and try to make it to the nearest settlement. Like
we talked about before."

Her eyes were wide with fear and understanding. She
clung to his hand. "Don't go, Rusty. I don't want anything to happen to you!"

"Now, now. I don't intend to let it. I'll take care of
you and me. But to do that, I've got to sneak up on
them." He put an arm around her and hugged her. "You
just do what I say, that's your job."

"All right, Rusty," she choked.

He stood up and looked down on her. "Can you do that? It will be a big help."

Mopping up her teary eyes with her sleeve, she tried to straighten her shoulders, "I can do it."

He went towards the woods, turned to give her a re-assuring smile, then disappeared.

Chapter Seventeen

Brisco knew only one way to wake up his associates, and that was to give them a swift kick in the ribs. On this particular morning, however, the kick was less sharp than others. He was, for once, almost in a good mood. This was his day. "Get up, you two! We've got a big day ahead of us!"

Farley blinked awake and looked about him. His eyes heavy with sleep, he pushed himself up into a sitting position with great difficulty. "Whadda ya doin'? It's still dark out."

Lem awoke before Brisco came over to him, but it did not save him from a kick. "Of course it's dark, you fools, we have to tackle McBride when he's asleep. Get up now!"

Lem crawled out of his blankets, shivering. He could

use that silver, sure enough. Get himself a nice little cabin before winter sets in. Hell, he was no kid anymore. His legs were stiff and his feet hurt from walking. All in all, he was feeling his age. Pulling on his damp boots, Lem reckoned he could kill right about now, without any qualms, for his share of McBride's silver. He looked at Brisco, who had already packed and was checking his precious 'hawk. He would have to keep an eye on him. He didn't want that 'hawk lodged in his own back.

Farley stumbled out of his blankets and reached for some wood. "What do you think you're doing?" Brisco asked sharply.

"It's cold and we gotta make somethin' to eat." Farley looked surprised at his question.

"Eat? We don't have time to eat! You can eat after we get that silver."

"But my stomach is plumb empty," Farley complained.

"So is your head! All we need is for McBride to see our campfire and you sitting next to it making breakfast! Pack your gear. We're moving out—now!"

Farley was about to object, but Lem shook his head at him behind Brisco's back. Resentfully, Farley got packed. "But ya know," he told Lem, "I ain't worth nothin' without some hot vittles in me."

Lem nodded. "Mebbe McBride will have somethin' worth eatin' when we catch up to him," he suggested. Farley brightened. "Sure now! He's got all them packs. Bound to be somethin' there."

Brisco led the way as usual. The other two had to hustle to keep up. As they neared McBride's camp, Brisco slowed down and stopped. When the two men came abreast of him, he laid out his plan. "That's his camp, right up ahead through the trees. Now this is how we're going in. Lem and Farley, you swing around to the left and take McBride. If he's asleep, pin him down and tie him up. I'll go in from the right and catch the girl."

The other two exchanged looks. "Why are you goin' after the girl?" Farley asked suspiciously. "Why not one of us?"

"Because you two fools would let her get away, that's why. That little kid is as slippery as an eel. She managed to get away from all of those Indians and I'm not trusting you two to catch her."

Lem got his pistol out and rechecked it. "I'll shoot McBride in the head while he's sleeping. It'll be faster that way," he said calmly.

"The hell you will!" Brisco snarled. "I want him alive!"

Lem looked at him coolly. "Better to kill him right off. Less trouble in the end."

"I'm giving orders around here and I say take him alive! Got it?"

Lem stuck his pistol back in his belt and gave Brisco a surly nod. He let his breath out in an angry noise as Brisco set off again, assuming his orders would be obeyed. Easy for him to say take McBride alive!

McBride was going to be one hell of a handful even with the two of them. Take him alive! He and Farley would be lucky if they came out of this in one piece!

"Why do ya reckon he wants him alive, Lem?" Farley asked. "Don't make no sense to me."

"'Cause he's mad as hell at him, that's why. This here trader shot him in the shoulder. See the way the bandage is bunched up under his shirt? McBride did that to him, cool as you please. I heard talk down at the settlement about it." Lem continued after a long moment, "Never a good thing to do somethin' in anger. Worse thing a body can do. Ya gotta hang on to yer temper or things get outta hand. Me now, I'd jest kill McBride right off. You tie him up, why that's jest waitin' fer trouble to happen. And if he kills that little kid while McBride is alive, who knows what he'll go and do. Maybe kill all of us! No sirree, kill him right off, that's what I say. Damn fool!" he muttered, glaring at Brisco's back.

Lem didn't have to worry. When they burst in on the camp, it was empty. Some embers still glowed in the fire, but everything else was gone.

Lem kneeled down and looked at the fire. "He built up that fire so that it would burn all night to fool us." Lem looked up at Brisco, who was staring blindly at the ashes as if he couldn't believe it. "Old Injun trick," Lem said flatly.

Suddenly, Brisco's face was suffused with livid color. Furiously, he kicked the dying fire, sending a spray of hot ashes into Lem's face.

"Damn it to hell! You crazy bastard!" Lem swore as he jumped up, swatting away burning cinders from his face and shirt.

Ignoring Lem's outrage, Brisco shouted, "They've gone!" His eyes twitched around the abandoned camp, looking about him, as if he could discover them lurking some place. Not content with standing still, he tore about erratically. His breathing was ragged as he found where the horses had been tied. The grass had been cropped short. They had been here! He couldn't believe it—he had been outmaneuvered. All his meticulously crafted plans of trapping McBride, killing him, and taking his silver, evaporated in angry reality. He had been duped!

"He musta known we was here," Lem stated. Brisco swung around.

"It was you two! Somehow one of you gave us away!" He took out his 'hawk and would have flung it, but Lem had his rifle ready.

"Put that down!" Brisco stopped with his 'hawk up over his head ready to hurl it. "Put it down, Brisco!" He cocked the hammer. Brisco's eyes seemed to clear a little. He lowered his 'hawk. "If anyone give us away, it was you. You were the one traipsing around here. Probably heard ya! So don't you go puttin' the blame on us!"

"He's right," Farley put in aggrieved. "We two were jest sittin' in the camp all night. We didn't go nowhere. It ain't fair you yellin' on us."

Lem could see how Brisco was struggling to rein in

his temper. He needed them, Lem thought cynically. Leastways, now he did. Lem had no illusions about Brisco. Brisco was smart enough to know that now was not the time to kill his partners. When his reason returned, he would realize that sure enough.

Brisco did. His grip on the 'hawk was so tight, his knuckles were white with the strain. Deliberately, he relaxed his hand. The rigidness left his body and he began to breathe more evenly. "That's right." Typical, Lem noticed, Brisco did not apologize, even for wanting to kill them!

"Maybe he doesn't even know we're on his trail," he mused aloud.

Lem personally thought that this was untrue, but he didn't voice his opinion. The black fury still clung to Brisco and would not abate until he'd killed his quarry. It was important for their safety to keep Brisco's anger honed in on McBride.

"Probably afeered of them Injuns," Lem remarked. He noticed, unhappily, how many little holes had been burned in his shirt by the ashes. He'd like to see Brisco buried in them ashes, he thought to himself. Tied to the stake, Injun-style, with his guts hanging out. Instead, he merely said, "Mebbe he ain't too far ahead. Mebbe we can catch up to him."

Brisco nodded as if this had already occurred to him.

"Seein' as he ain't here, how about some breakfast?" Farley asked plaintively. "I'm all hollow." He stopped as Brisco swung around on him.

"We're not eating until we find McBride! Pick up your packs and let's get out of here!" He turned on his heel and left the camp practically running, trying to find the trail. Lem and Farley followed more slowly.

Two hours later, they still hadn't found a sign of McBride. Brisco's face was set in ominous lines. "Don't tell me he doesn't know we're following him! How else does he know to keep so well-hidden?"

"Indians!" Lem said suddenly, noticing a hoof print in the dirt. Brisco came up and kneeled next to Lem to get a better look. "No wonder he's bein' so careful," Lem added in a conciliatory tone.

Brisco gave a noncommittal grunt then pointed out, "There's more over there."

"They look pretty recent," Lem said speculatively. "Mebbe we should lie low for a while."

Brisco turned his head to look at him. "Shut up! We're moving! I want to get him before those Indians do!"

Lem stood up, unhappily. It was hard enough trying to nail down McBride without them damned Indians swarming all over the place.

"What if them Injuns git him first?" Farley asked Lem as they followed Brisco. "What if they get the silver afore us? What then? Whole week wasted."

"Aw, shut up," Lem said disgustedly. "I wish I never come!"

Rusty backtracked over his own trail. He knew once Brisco and his accomplices picked up his sign, they would stick closer to it than a flea on a dog. He didn't waste his time in anger or resentment at what they were doing. It was part of life out here. Once you accepted that there was little to stand between you and death except yourself, you simply learned to be cautious.

Rusty smiled grimly. He wondered how many so-called "civilized" people would stoop to crime if there was no court to enforce the laws. Out here, you just naturally saw what people were really like. Some, like Joe Wilder, would bring law and order with his club no matter where he happened to live. Others, like the jackal Brisco, sunk to the lowest level permitted. It wasn't up to Rusty to teach him. All he wanted to do was to make sure Isabelle and the silver were safe. Some people, he mused, just couldn't live peaceably with other human beings. Brisco was one of them.

Rusty was being painstakingly thorough. He made a large circle, hoping he had traveled far enough to come up behind the three men. There was no doubt in his mind that they were out there someplace. Even the signs of Indians didn't make Rusty ease up on his hunt for the men. He had kept up a breakneck pace this past day, so he figured he had about a mile or two lead on them. He was right. About an hour later, he came upon them.

Rusty was in luck. Just as he had hoped, the men were strung out. Brisco, like a hound impatient for the hunt, was far in the lead. Lem was next and Farley, being slower and heavier, lagged back. Rusty moved around all three, then came up behind the last man and waited for his chance.

Exhausted by the killing pace, Farley stopped for a moment to catch his breath. The others disappeared from view as the foliage closed behind them. Tuckered out, he leaned his rifle against a tree as if it was too heavy for him, shut his eyes, and rested. Rusty came up silently behind him.

"Farley?" he said in a low voice.

"Huh?" Farley's eyes flew open and he turned around. That's when the heavy butt of a wooden rifle came slamming into his forehead. Farley grunted in pain. The butt rammed again into his fleshy, vulnerable stomach. Groaning, he doubled over and fell with a loud thud to the ground.

Quick as a cat, Rusty stood over his inert body and trussed him up with strips of leather. Then he rolled him over and hid him in the underbrush. Picking up Farley's rifle, he put the ammunition in his pouch and tossed the rifle into the woods. He then commenced to stalk Lem.

Lem wouldn't be so easy to take. He was smarter than Farley, wily, and fast on his feet.

Up ahead, Lem kept looking back for his friend. "I don't see Farley," he called to Brisco, who was not checking to see if the other two were close behind. The man didn't seem to tire, Lem thought nastily. He sure was in an all-fired hurry to lift some scalps.

"Keep moving! He'll just have to keep up," Brisco said sharply. "We can't let them get too far ahead."

Lem obeyed him for a while, but it was clear he was getting worried. With a glance at Brisco's back, he began slowing down. When Brisco was out of sight, he stopped. He looked back. No Farley. Damn his eyes! Probably resting some place. They had been walking for nearly twelve hours without a break. He was about to drop in his tracks himself. Farley, who was not so good on his feet, probably had already.

At that moment, he heard a noise in the woods. At last! "Farley?" he asked tartly. "Get along here!" He squinted as the sun shone in his eyes then he took a few steps toward the noise. "Danged if I don't—"

Rusty never found out what he was danged about, because the butt of his rifle came crashing down on Lem's forehead. Lem saw bright lights. Then he saw Rusty.

"I knew it! I knew you were on to us!" he muttered.

"You were right, Lem." Rusty smiled before bringing the rifle up and smashing it into Lem's chin. His head jerked as he fell backwards onto the ground, and he was out cold. Rusty tied him up and took his ammunition for himself. He tossed the rifle into the trees.

Rusty had to hurry now. Even though he had dispatched the two men in good time, he knew that James Brisco was the real threat. Unable to feel any kind of human emotions, Brisco was nevertheless able to read them in others—to his advantage. Brisco for instance, would know that Isabelle, not the silver, was now Rusty's primary concern. He couldn't appreciate it, would even deride it, but he would understand it and use it.

Sacrificing caution for speed, Rusty made for the boulder field where he told Isabelle to slow up. He wanted to get there before Brisco did and position himself. He had seen that Brisco had been a long way ahead of the others. Somehow, Rusty didn't think he was going to slow down and wait for them. Brisco was chomping at the bit, eager for action.

Rusty knew that Brisco would take Isabelle, not the silver, first. Even if he could wrest the horses away from her and leave, he wouldn't do that. He wanted revenge. What better revenge than to capture Little Bit, then make Rusty watch while he killed her! Farley and Lem, you might deal with, but Brisco—never! Killing was not only a necessity to him, but a pleasure as well.

As he neared the rocks, Rusty slowed down to catch his breath. Finding some thick bushes, he halted and took cover. At first there was no noise. Only the low buzz of insects rang in his ears. Gradually, the humming was replaced by the customary forest sounds. Where was Isabelle? Had she even made it this far? Had Brisco caught up with her? Maybe she had lost her way. Was she even now his hostage? With dreadful care, Rusty held himself still.

Slowly, Rusty's eyes scanned the forest, looking for some movement or sign to indicate the presence of his enemy. His ears strained for the least sound while he continued to hold his rifle ready to be used.

Had Brisco gone back to get his friends? If he had, that would buy Rusty more time. Good luck in finding them. Even if he did, they would be in no condition to be of much help. Hopefully, Rusty had given them a distaste for the job. Rusty didn't think he had gone back, however. If Brisco thought he could take Rusty by himself, he would do it. Then he wouldn't even have to make a pretense of sharing with the others.

Then he heard it: a soft clumping ahead, like a horse shifting its feet.

Rusty's nerves were wound tight. It was a trap! He could feel it. Yet he couldn't see or hear anything suspicious. Easing closer, he caught sight of Isabelle and the horses. They were stopped, as he had instructed her to do, in the boulder field. He smiled briefly. She had positioned herself between two packhorses. All you could see of her was the brown calico of her dress and the new moccasins peeking out from underneath. *Smart little kid!* He had no doubt that she was frightened— probably listening like he was for some sound she could recognize.

But there was no sound—at first. Rusty had to quell the urge to rush over and reassure her. Something was not right. As he watched, he saw Isabelle pat the horses and speak gently to them. She was trying to comfort herself as much as them, he knew instinctively.

Swish.

Rusty saw the horse's head move convulsively as if a small hand had jerked on the rein. Rusty tensed.

Swish.

It had a secretive, sly sound to it.

"Little girl." A cold, sinister voice spoke flatly in the forest. Isabelle didn't move a muscle. "I can see you between the horses. Come out here or I'll cut your friend, McBride, to rags when I see him."

It was an emotionless voice. Isabelle didn't doubt him in the least. Slowly, she leaned down and saw the buckskin pants from underneath the belly of the horse. She also saw the rifle, held in a businesslike manner. She could make a run for it as Rusty had told her, but Isabelle didn't think she could make it. Besides, loyal little soul that she was, she couldn't leave Rusty by himself. She started to straighten up again, but before she did, she picked up a nice-sized rock. Holding it in the folds of her skirt, Isabelle came out slowly.

Don't do it, Rusty fumed to himself. Brisco wouldn't dare shoot her. He couldn't take the chance of hitting one of the horses. That would make it impossible for him to pack out all of the silver. Isabelle didn't think of this. All her thoughts were of how she could protect Rusty. As she came out, Rusty took advantage of Brisco's temporary distraction to move in close.

"Where's McBride?" his voice rapped out, cutting across her thoughts.

"I don't know, sir," she answered politely. As she replied, her eyes briefly flickered around to where Rusty was crouched by a tree just behind Brisco. Their eyes met for an instant. He gave her full credit for not giving him away by any change in her expression. Instead, she fixed her eyes firmly on Brisco who was becoming annoyed.

"You know where he is, you little brat! What did he tell you? What did you two plan? Are you supposed to meet him here?" His eyes swept the large field of boulders that surrounded them. "Easy place to find." His face darkened unpleasantly as he leveled his gun at her. "If you don't tell me, I'm going to shoot you!" At her silence, he became infuriated. "Speak up! Where's McBride?"

"Right behind you."

Brisco swiveled around, bringing his rifle up. Rusty moved in. With great presence of mind, Isabelle hurled her rock straight at Brisco's head. The rock found its target first. It smacked into Brisco's temple, throwing off his aim. The gun exploded harmlessly in the air.

Suddenly, Rusty was there, slamming the butt of his rifle into Brisco's chest, then smashing it upwards, into his chin.

Snarling with pain, Brisco fell back, holding his aching jaw. Brisco was enraged. One minute he had the silver within his grasp and the girl in his sights. He hadn't even heard the ex-ranger come up behind him! A vain man, he had assumed the young trader was naively unaware that he was being followed. The absence of his companions he had attributed to their own stupidity. It suddenly hit him that McBride had planned this all. McBride had gotten rid of Lem and Farley— and now he intended to get rid of him!

His eyes were wild with pent-up rage. As he stood there, panting and touching his jaw, he rasped out,

"That's going to cost you, McBride! First, I'll take you apart, then the kid!"

He moved in, but McBride was faster.

Rusty shoved his fist into Brisco's stomach before Brisco came back and walloped him with a wicked right jab to his left eye. Teeth bared, he began pummeling Rusty's head and body with his hard, bony fists. It was the action of a man gone mad.

Rusty tried to dodge and protect himself, but Brisco was like an unleashed beast. All he could think of was that he had been outwitted.

Rusty doubled up from a jolting blow to his ribs. Brisco brought his fist in a smashing uppercut to Rusty's face. Blood spurted from Rusty's nose and his eye began to swell up. He tried to hit blindly back but came only on empty air.

Isabelle, jumping up and down excitedly during the fight, saw with horror that her hero was losing! Hunting around, she found another rock. It was small enough for her to lift but large enough to do damage. She looked for her chance and got it. As Brisco's hand shot out to grab Rusty by the front of his buckskin shirt, Isabelle banged the rock down hard on Brisco's foot. It made a satisfying crunch that went right through his moccasins.

Swearing incoherently, Brisco kicked out at Isabelle, grazing the side of her head. As she stumbled backwards, he turned once more to Rusty, who was getting his second wind. Brisco's hand snaked down to his boot where he kept his knife sheathed. Isabelle saw this and scooted over on hands and knees behind him. As he grasped the hilt, she bit him hard and drew blood.

"You little—"

He tried to backhand her and the knife flew out of his grip several feet. Rusty came alive. Bringing his knee up, he drove it sharply into Brisco's stomach. As the man gasped, Rusty lowered his head and smashed jolting blows into the other man's ribs and stomach. With one vicious slug, he could feel bones crack and give. Gasping for breath, Rusty knew he had to take him down now—all the way. It wasn't enough just to wound him. He had to make sure that he couldn't walk away from this fight—literally. Or crawl for that matter, Rusty thought. He had to be stopped now or Isabelle wouldn't be safe.

His muscles ached, his left eye was turning purple, his knuckles were bruised and bleeding, but Rusty kept punching. With all his weight, Rusty threw a wicked uppercut. That final blow seemed to do it. Brisco's eyes were becoming glassy and the insane fire that had burned within them was beginning to diminish. Now that the end was in sight, Rusty hoped the other two men wouldn't show up at the last moment to help their comrade. Brisco was more than enough for one man to deal with.

All of a sudden, Brisco shook off his stupor and lunged, knocking Rusty hard to the ground. Brisco lifted his leg to stomp him in the stomach, but Rusty managed to catch hold of his foot and shoved. The shove sent Brisco staggering back against a huge tree trunk. It knocked the wind out of him but, as Rusty rolled to his feet, Brisco was already swinging. He wound back his fist, driving it with all his considerable strength at Rusty's jaw. It was a last, desperate attempt to subdue his adversary. Had it connected, it would have leveled him.

Using both hands, Rusty grabbed the closed fist and twisted it viciously. He heard a sickening snap. Brisco screamed like an injured animal and toppled to the ground.

Rusty watched him for a few seconds as he lay motionless. Taking great gulps of air, he got up and kicked the fallen man in the side. It was not because he was vindictive but, like a snake, you never knew if he was pretending. Rusty had nothing to fear. Brisco was unconscious.

"You did it, Rusty! You did it!" Isabelle rushed to him and hugged his knees, all she could reach. "I knew you'd get him all along. I only pretended to worry."

Still breathing heavily, Rusty said, "Let's tie him up." Isabelle eagerly ran to find some pieces of rawhide. Rusty bound him tightly, notwithstanding his broken arm and cracked ribs.

Afterwards, he put his hand on her shining blond head. "Did he hurt you, Isabelle? I saw him kick out." He touched his own jaw gingerly. "He packs quite a wallop."

"Oh no," she scoffed. "But I got him!"

"You sure did! You were a big help. I couldn't have done it without you, Little Bit." Isabelle beamed at such praise from her hero.

"What are you going to do with the varmint? Are we taking him with us? He'll be an awful lot of trouble."

He grinned through his bloody lips. "You're right, Little Bit. And I wouldn't trust him, even with one broken arm and tied up like a calf. We'll leave him here. If his friends find him, they're welcome to him."

Isabelle saw nothing wrong with this. Dismissing Brisco, she got some water and insisted on washing away the blood. He sat patiently through her awkward ministrations.

"Thank you," he said gravely. "I feel a lot better," he lied. To tell the truth, he felt like hell warmed over, if that was possible. It would be nice to camp right here and get some much needed sleep, but he didn't want to chance Brisco's friends coming on them. They still might have an appetite for silver. Moreover, he didn't want to be anywhere near this place when they unloosed Brisco. It would be like cutting loose the devil.

He told Isabelle to get ready to move out. "We can't stop here." Then he went up to Brisco. His eyes were open and glaring malevolently at Rusty.

"You bastard! No one's ever beaten me yet—and lived!" His face was still a bloody mess. Isabelle had not offered to clean it.

"Now, is that a nice word to use in front of a young lady?"

"Yes, it's a bad word." Isabelle wagged her finger at him as if he was a disobedient child. Rusty noticed uneasily how his eyes flashed hate. The disdainful act enraged him.

"When I get hold of you, little girl, I'm going to—"

Here, Rusty gave him a swift kick. It effectively cut off the threats.

"Enough of that," Rusty said. "You just concentrate on how you're going to get out of here. And if you do, don't come to the fort. I'm going to lay my complaint before the colonel. If you show up, you and your friends will be hanged."

At these words, Brisco's face changed. "You're not taking me with you? You're just leaving me tied up like this in the middle of nowhere?"

"It does seem harsh," Rusty agreed. "After all, you only tried to kill Isabelle and me, and scalp us, and dump our bodies in the river so everyone would think the Indians did it. Then you'd take our silver."

Brisco's eyes opened wide with fury as he realized that Rusty had been listening in at their camp two evenings back.

"You were there?" His voice was deadly cold. "I could have killed you right there! It would have been easy!" His teeth gritted as he realized the chance he had missed. McBride had been eavesdropping on them! He had heard their whole plan. No wonder he had been gone the next morning.

"Yes, it would have. Lucky for me you were too busy listening to your good friends plotting to kill you. Nothing more heartwarming than thieves planning how to kill each other."

"If I meet up with you again—"

"If I see you again, I'll shoot first and this time I'll kill you." Squatting down next to Brisco, Rusty grabbed a fistful of hair and jerked his head back so Brisco could see his hard, green eyes. There was no mistaking the steel-edged danger in them. "Remember that, Brisco." He leaned forward so Isabelle couldn't hear. "If that little girl wasn't along you would be lying there with a bullet in your head and your scalp in my pouch. So don't expect me to go holding you by the hand all the way to the fort. You're alive. It's more than you deserve for what you were planning to do. Maybe the Indians will find you or maybe your friends will. You'll probably end up dead either way."

"Am I supposed to be grateful?" he sneered.

"I don't expect much of anything from you." He let go of Brisco roughly, then stood up. "Come on, Isabelle."

She took up Bessie's rope and followed. "Good-bye, Mr. Brisco," she said politely. He swore back.

"Let's get along. Those friends of his might be back," Rusty said as they rounded a bend and were out of earshot.

"What did you do to them? Did you kill them?"

"No, just knocked them out and tied them up."

"Oh." She sighed disappointedly. She followed after Rusty, without giving a further thought to the bloody, broken, man who had tried to kill them. Isabelle had a strong streak of practicality in her.

Chapter Eighteen

Molly touched Ben's sleeve gently and asked, "How long do you think it will be before we get to our valley, Ben?"

"Probably tomorrow. I thought we would go past Bewilderness first. Let people know what happened. Maybe get more supplies." Then, Ben remembered he had little money. Molly just nodded. It bothered him that he didn't have much to offer except his own hard work. The Fletchers didn't have much either, but it was still more than he had.

"I can build a lean-to while the cabin is being built, and you and your father can sleep in the wagon." He sounded almost apologetic. Dammit, he scolded himself angrily, he was a hard worker! And out here, that counted for more than a wagonload of useless possessions. For all the goods they carried, those people on the wagon train couldn't help themselves when adversity struck.

There were other skills he possessed, too, like a knowledge of the wilderness and the ability to find game where game was scarce. He was handy with tools and could build a fine home for himself. He was well equipped to provide for a wife and family. A damned sight better than most!

Then he stopped cold. Ever since he met up with the Fletchers, his mind kept rambling down the same path. Sure, he had thought about marriage before, but it was always sometime off in the future with a girl he could only imagine. But Molly was here, now, and she gave him a lot to mull over.

"Ben," Molly broke into his thoughts. "You don't have to build a lean-to. We have plenty of room in the wagon, once everything is moved out."

"We'll see." Ben turned away, embarrassed. "Why don't you go up and work the brake?" He liked being near her too much and Mr. Fletcher might frown on it. After all, they were going to be partners. He wanted Aaron to trust him. Anyway, he'd have to earn his own money first, before—here his thoughts broke off as he realized where they were leading again.

Share a wagon with her! That'll be the day! Just the thought of it made him sweat. He couldn't count how many sleepless hours he'd spent thinking about Molly.

Tucked away in his bedroll under the wagon, he would lay awake long into the night, tortured by the thought of her sleeping just above him.

And there were things she did that made his temperature soar and his heartbeat quicken. Like the time he had caught a glimpse of the hem of her nightgown! That had just about done him in. It happened at dawn when he'd heard the wagon bed creak. His eyes flew open. Then he saw her. She had climbed out of the wagon early to fetch her shoes drying by the fire. Being wrapped tightly from neck to foot in a blanket did nothing to hide her shapely figure, or the tantalizing bit of white linen swirling around her neat ankles. Ben tried to look away but was mesmerized by the bewitching vision.

When she leaned over to pick up her shoes, her eyes cut sideways to where he was sleeping. Ben had squeezed his eyes shut, but he could feel her watching him for several never-ending moments. Then she straightened up. As she stole back to her bed on tiptoe, totally unaware of his interest as any well-bred young lady would, he sneaked a forbidden glimpse of her again.

When he finally heard her settle back into her covers, Ben rolled onto his back, exhaling his pent-up breath. Staring at the wagon above him, he ran a nervous hand through his hair. It was fast becoming a worrisome situation.

"Ben?" Aaron called. "Why don't we stop for the afternoon? I could use a rest. Can you find us a place up ahead?" Ben nodded, glad to leave his turbulent thoughts alone for a spell. He soon outpaced the others and located a quiet little meadow tucked away among a circle of trees.

As Molly got the supper going, Ben unhitched the team. They were restless, pulling at the tether. Their ears perked up and their heads turned towards the trail they had just left.

Walking away from them on the soft, mossy ground, Ben stopped and stared into the dappled woods. Tense and still, he listened, but no sound met his ears.

Slowly his gaze swept the camp: Molly kneeling by the fire, Aaron sitting on a log drinking a cup of water. They were both making small, familiar little noises, but the horses didn't look. Their attention was glued to the forest beyond Ben's shoulders.

A dark shadow moved among the trees.

Instantly, Ben snapped his rifle to his shoulder and began backing up towards the others.

"Get out of the way, Molly! Aaron, get your gun!" he ordered in a low, intense voice. Molly stared at him, startled, then noticed his eyes playing over the thick forest directly in front of them. Dropping the pot by the fire, she grabbed her rifle and leaped behind the huge log on which her father had been sitting. Aaron moved fast for an ailing man! He snatched up his rifle and crouched down next to his daughter. With his free hand, he shoved Molly down further and aimed his rifle at the expanse of blackness. Ben had positioned himself by the wagon.

Now Molly could hear a shuffling noise and it was getting louder. Whoever it was, was moving purposefully towards them, making no effort to disguise their movements.

"Hello at the campsite!" a man's voice called out. At the edge of the woods a dark figure loomed up followed by another. Ben leveled his rifle at the first form.

"Aaron, take the second man." Then Ben shouted out, "Stop right there, mister!"

"Hold on there, young feller. I'll come in real slow." It was a man's voice and, by the sound of it, an old one. Sure enough, the man who stepped into the light was an old relic—seventy years if he was a day. But Ben knew how crafty these old codgers could be. He kept his rifle on him till the stranger came into camp and Ben got a good look at him.

He had a grizzled beard with a battered hat pulled down on his graying head. The second figure was a horse laden with furs.

"Don't shoot! I'm friendly! So's Matilda!" To prove it, he gave a big smile. He had broken and blackened teeth, but it was a cheery smile that alleviated everyone's fears.

"Just happened to smell that thar stew and thought I'd ask if you'd be kind enough to share it. Name's Nash Winslow." Ben had heard of him. He was a trapper who made Bewilderness his center of operation.

Mr. Fletcher spoke up. "Good evening, Mr. Winslow. My name is Fletcher. This is my daughter, Molly, and our friend, Ben Allyn. Come and set a spell, and bring Matilda."

The man tethered his horse to the wagon wheel, then lowered himself down heavily on a large rock near the fire. "Pleased ta meet ya. Ma'am." He nodded to Molly. "I'm takin' my furs to trade. Had me a purty hot time of it, dodgin' them Injuns! It was touch and go for a while there. But I come through it all intact."

Molly got another bowl and dished out some stew and a thick slice of bread to go with it. Winslow's eyes gleamed.

"Thank you, young lady. Now I call that real friendly!" He took a mouthful and made sounds of pleasure. "Now that's good eatin'! If I was ten years younger, I'd marry ya, little miss!" Molly smiled, but Ben did not look amused. Then Winslow looked at Ben.

"Always marry a girl who can cook, son. When the kissin' is gone, the cookin' is still there!" A pink-faced Molly dished out the stew to the others. As she handed Ben his plate, her eyes flitted quickly to his, then away again when she saw the speculative look in them. It was clear to see he was thinking more about the kissin' than the cookin'.

Before they had finished, Nash was asking for more. "Fine eatin'! Fine eatin'! And tea too!" His watery-blue eyes were eager as Molly handed him a cup of Mrs. Miller's tea.

"Give him a nice, brimming cupful, Molly." Ben's lips twitched as he spoke.

"Maybe two cups of it," Aaron added, elbowing Ben. Winslow drank it down greedily. Ben smiled, and Mr. Fletcher tried not to. Both waited for him to spit out the vile tasting stuff, but he swallowed it down and kept it down. Instead of grimacing, he smacked his lips. Aaron and Ben were chagrined.

"If I didn't know better, I'd say that was Dr. Mungo's restorative tea! Yes sirree. Tastes just like it!"

"It is!" Molly replied, startled. "Would you like some more?"

"More? I'll say! That thar tea will cure you of everything from gout to colic." He drank the rest with great gusto.

"Pa was sick with fever and he had some. He's much better now," Molly offered.

"There ya are. Another testimonial! That Dr. Mungo sure knows his onions!" Then he picked up the slab of corn bread, held it to his nose and inhaled deeply before biting off a healthy chunk. "Corn bread too. It's a good thing I come upon upon you folks." Nash ate the corn bread and accepted the last knob of it that Molly unwillingly offered. When he was sure there was no more food to be had, he leaned back, happy and replete.

"Looks like ya got into a fight," Aaron remarked, noting the dark blue mark on his cheek. Winslow touched it gingerly.

"Met up with a weasel. Weasel by the name of Kenny Minks." Ben started. Molly and Aaron both stared at Ben. "Yes sirree, I sure am lucky. First I tackle Kenny Minks, and now I get some restorative tea. What a day!"

"Kenny Minks?" Ben asked slowly. "I've been hunting for him myself."

"Well, if ya look hard you'll find little pieces of him back there." He laughed heartily, thrusting his big thumb towards the south. "That cheatin' skunk took off with my pack of hides here. Thought to sell them and keep the money. But I got him first. Beat him to a pulp with the butt of my rifle." He paused. "I think I musta broke some of his bones 'cause he was in real bad shape when I left him lyin' in the woods. He won't never steal from this old coot agin! Probably could use a sip of that tea right about now!" He laughed.

"Did he say anything about some canoes?"

"No, son. He didn't have time to say anythin'. I didn't give him a chance. I just up and clubbed him afore he could say 'Howdy.' Not that he would have, anyway. He knowed why I was there. He just didn't think I'd catch up with him. But I did." Winslow said it with great satisfaction.

"He stole some canoes from Ben without paying for them," Molly put in indignantly.

"That a fact? Well, he probably got rid of them for money already. Leastways, he wasn't draggin' them along in the woods." He gaffawed at this, slapping his thigh. Ben wasn't amused. "Tell ya what, son. If ya want to get a piece of him, you'll probably find him a-moanin' and a-groanin' back there 'bout a mile and a half thet-away." He nodded southwards with his head.

Molly looked anxiously at Ben. She didn't want him to to leave. Not now. Not ever. She didn't want him to beat anybody up just out of anger. Not even a no-account bounder like Minks. Her smooth brow wrinkled in dismay. But she knew she had no right to stop him. Molly looked at her father, alarm clearly registering on her face. Maybe he could say something to stop Ben. What about their valley? Their dreams? Aaron saw her panic. He opened his mouth to speak, then shut it. This was the lad's decision, not his. He had to make it by himself and live with it.

Ben looked down at the ground awhile, considering his options. His serious young gaze settled on Molly for a moment. He knew which path he would take and it would be with Molly. Then he looked over at Nash Winslow.

"I don't think I'll go after him. Those canoes don't seem so important now." He glanced back at Molly and saw her smile with pure pleasure. Aaron relaxed. Everything was going to be just fine.

The old man grinned hugely, winking at Molly. "Don't blame ya, son. Don't blame ya a bit!"

Chapter Nineteen

After leaving Brisco to his fate, all trussed up and scorching mad, Rusty kept on for the rest of the day and well into the night. His body was a mass of weariness but he moved on. Finally exhausted, they made camp in a small valley.

One thing was certain. When he got to Fort Pitt, he was going to sleep for a week. He hated to admit it to himself but Brisco had really worked him over. His left eye was rimmed with purple. He touched his jaw tenderly. He had taken a hard punch there. In fact, his entire body ached from Brisco's vicious body slams.

Rusty looked down at his hands. The swelling was beginning to go down now, but for a while he had lost his grip. In a hand-to-hand fight anyone could take him down easily. He hoped the situation wouldn't arise.

They were almost there, only a few days out of Fort Pitt, and Rusty was feeling pretty pleased with how things were working out. He, Isabelle, and the silver would get to the fort after all. Rusty knew there were times when he seriously doubted they would.

He had hated playing sitting duck for Brisco and his men. Turning the tables on them, hunting them down one by one—that had been a risky proposition. It could have backfired right in his face, leaving him and Isabelle in Brisco's pitiless hands. It still made his skin crawl when he considered the ultimate high stakes he had been playing for.

All along he had tried not to signal his fears to Little Bit, but she was sharp and seemed to understand instinctively the perils of his situation.

Still, they weren't in the clear yet. And he had to keep up the vigil.

"Let me know if you hear anything," he told Little Bit as they took to their blankets. "Brisco might still be following." Isabelle didn't worry. She knew that no matter how many men came, Rusty McBride would take care of them all.

The next day they went slower. It was a cool, sunny day and for the first time Rusty began to feel that they weren't being pursued—not right now anyway. Lem and Farley, he might not see again, but Brisco was different. If he got out alive, Rusty knew he would come after him.

Brisco was not the kind of man to let a beating go

unpunished. An intelligent man would shrug and cut his losses. But not Brisco. He did not operate by intelligence even though he possessed it. What drove him was the unrelenting need to get back at all of those who got the better of him. He was a man who truly wanted to say that there was no one alive who had beaten him.

Well, no use worrying about Brisco, Rusty thought. What would come in the future wasn't anything even James Brisco could predict. Right now, the silver was on his mind—and the Indians. Where were they now? Where had they gone once they attacked the wagon train? Rusty had been sidetracked a little, but they were still about, he was sure. That night, he found out exactly where they were.

Just as Isabelle had finished washing the dishes and Rusty had gotten out their blankets, he heard his horses mince nervously where they stood, tethered. He suddenly knew who was out there. Before he could make a move, four forms materialized noiselessly out of the dark forest. Rusty cursed himself for building a fire, even a small one. Now he had put Isabelle, and his own life, in jeopardy. He had not doubted it was the light that attracted them to his camp.

In the flickering flames he could see their hawkish, painted faces. He knew they had been part of the war party. He did not have to see the scalps, freshly tanned and hanging from their belts, to realize that.

As always, he had his rifle to hand. Knowing that showing fear meant instant death, he greeted them solemnly. As he did so, he gently shoved Isabelle behind him. At least he could give her a head start if she had to run for it.

They exchanged greetings ceremoniously and squatted down on their heels. Their hard black eyes flicked around, searching the darkness for the packhorses concealed behind a flimsy corral of branches. They knew McBride carried goods because the hooves cut deep tracks from the heavy load. They had no idea most of the freight was silver.

Rusty sat down again on a stump with his rifle across his knees. With seeming casualness he aimed the rifle at the old warrior's stomach. His finger lightly played with the trigger. The men took this in at a glance but their enigmatic expressions didn't change. They looked into the flinty depths of the white man's eyes. He wouldn't hesitate to shoot.

The old man was their spokesman and came to the point. Many of their braves had been killed, he said, and they needed goods to cover the dead. Rusty had dealt with Indians before. If you gave them enough goods, they let you live. If not . . .

Rusty said that although he didn't have many goods with him, he would share what he had with his brothers. He went to his packs and gave them sugar, salt, bacon, knives and tobacco, which he stacked before them. They were displeased and wanted more.

This was a touchy situation. Rusty carefully explained that he had no more to give them, but after he reached Fort Pitt and bought more goods, he could give more to his brothers. They could come to his trading post if they liked. They knew well enough of Rusty McBride and his trading post, he was sure.

They stared at him for a long time, and Rusty knew they were considering whether he was lying and whether it might be easier just to kill him and take all of the goods. A chill ran through him as he waited for their decision.

"I have something." Isabelle broke the menacing silence. She had watched the proceedings with wide eyes. Isabelle reached down for her small pack that contained her things, and took out a brown bag.

"No!" Rusty blurted out as she stepped around him. He reached out for her but she had already placed herself between him and the braves. Instantly, there was a spark in the old warrior's eyes. They both knew the girl had made a potentially deadly mistake.

Rusty raised his rifle to zero in on the old man's heart. The old warrior's lips twitched with amusement at the white man's unspoken threat.

Shyly, Isabelle went up to the old warrior and, unflinchingly, looked into the fierce face streaked with vermillion. She took his hand and opened the fingers, one by one. The Indians looked mystified. Then she took out a piece of candy and pressed it into his palm. She went to the next one and put candy in his hand. The last two, seeing what she was doing, opened their hands and waited for her to give them candy. When she was finished she took one herself, held it up between two fingers so they could see, and put it into her mouth. "Ummm," she said, indicating that it was good, and patted her stomach.

The old warrior put the candy into his mouth. He must have enjoyed it because he started to smile and said "Ummm" loudly. The others followed suit. Suddenly they were all laughing and saying "Ummm" and rubbing their stomachs. Their good humor once more restored, they got up to leave clutching their goods.

The old warrior turned once more to Rusty, his narrowed, now expressionless eyes revealing nothing. Then he looked at Isabelle and said "Ummm" solemnly. Isabelle took another candy out and handed it to him. He took it from her then detached a small doeskin bag from his belt and gave it to her. She smiled happily and curtsied. He gave a barking laugh, shot a penetrating sidelong look at Rusty, then vanished into the darkness as suddenly as he had appeared.

When they were out of sight, Rusty didn't waste a second. He began packing. There was a chance their good mood would evaporate and they would decide to attack him after all. Rusty wanted to be as far away from that cold-eyed wolf as possible. They left more than two miles between them and the Indians before they made camp. This time, he did not make the mistake of lighting a fire.

As he made her bed up Rusty said, "Little girl, you just saved us again." Then he shook his head. "But don't you ever get between the enemy and my rifle again!"

"Yes, Rusty. But Rusty, don't you think that Indian was a nice man? He gave me a pretty beaded bag."

"Oh, sure. Charming dinner guests he and his friends make!" She nodded in agreement. "I guess I'll have to remember to stock up on candy. I got a hunch they'll be expecting it from now on."

"Do you really think I helped?" Isabelle asked earnestly.

"You sure did."

"Do you think I've been a help all along?"

An alarm bell went off in Rusty's head, but he couldn't identify the source. "You sure have been. I don't know how I could have come this far without you."

"And . . . and you don't mind my company?"

"I like it." He patted her head. "It's kind of lonely traveling by myself."

She gave a great big smile. "Then you think I could go back with you and help you at your trading post?"

For once Rusty was speechless. *So that's where those questions were headed.* "Trading post?"

"You said I helped." She came to sit next to him on the log. "I can do a lot more too. I'm strong, see?" She held out her thin arm. "I'm a real hard worker." There was desperation in her voice.

"What about your aunt and uncle?"

"They don't want me." She lowered her voice. "They

never even wrote back to the lawyer. He just sent me anyway, because he didn't want to be bothered. I'll be good, Rusty. And I'll do whatever you want and I won't complain. And I won't eat much."

"We'll have to see," Rusty said weakly, hating the way the blue eyes brightened at his words.

For a long time Rusty laid there thinking. He liked Little Bit a lot. Someday he'd like to have a daughter like her. But she had kin. An aunt and uncle. No doubt they would be delighted to have her, she was such a likable little scrap. Besides, she needed a woman to mother her, not a bachelor who knew nothing at all about raising children and girls in particular. Somehow the idea daunted him. He comforted himself with the cheering thought that once she saw her kinfolk, she would change her mind. That's what she'd do, Rusty reassured himself. No need worrying now. Tomorrow would take care of his problems. Still not entirely comfortable, he turned into his blanket.

Chapter Twenty

As they neared Bewilderness, Molly was walking up ahead. Aaron Fletcher, now strong enough to ride, was mounted on the lead horse. Ben brought up the rear. Soon, very soon, Ben thought, they would get to the valley. Then what? This problem had been perplexing him for the last few miles.

This morning when Molly was out of hearing distance, Ben had shyly broached the subject to Aaron. What weighed on his mind most was his lack of money. He wanted to make his financial position clear to Aaron from the start. He found the older man seated in the wagon puffing contentedly on his pipe. Without preamble he began. It was no use putting off the inevitable with a lot of useless small talk.

"You know, sir, I was supposed to have money from

Kenny Minks for making those canoes," he began with heightened color. "I worked hard for weeks but I don't have much spare money right now to show for it. Maybe you don't want to go into partnership with me yet. I can understand that. Maybe you would rather wait until I earned my share. I could do some trapping this winter or try to get a job with the survey team at the settlement."

Aaron was alarmed and dismayed, but his expressionless face didn't betray this. Money was a delicate subject at any time and with anyone, but Ben was particularly sensitive about it. He seemed to be ashamed to be sharing their food even though he had contributed to the pot with some fish and small game.

Dammit, he liked the lad! If he had a son, he would have wanted him to be as forthright and honest as the young man standing before him. He admired Ben. It took a man to admit his shortcomings when it was plain to see the boy wanted this partnership more than anything.

Ben was clutching his felt hat, crumpling it out of shape as he stood there waiting for Aaron to respond. Aaron looked into Ben's crestfallen, anxious face. The boy needed assurance. He must handle this very delicately.

"To tell the truth, son, we ain't got much either," he confided. "Only I wasn't man enough to speak first. I should have said somethin' though. It was cowardly of me. I was afraid it might put you off. But the truth is plain enough. If we help each other we'll get through the winter fine. Land is free, and it ain't money that will get that cabin built afore winter or clear the land for spring planting. I was sort of hoping that if we helped each other, why, that would be a fair trade. But maybe," he said quietly, "you think you'd get the worse of it, having to do most of the work till I'm my old self again."

"Oh, no," Ben hurriedly reassured him. "The thought never entered my head!"

"I admit I haven't been much help up to now, but when that restorative tea takes hold"—he smiled—"I'll be doin' my fair share. Won't nothin' stop me then!"

Ben's face softened a fraction.

"But I have an idea and it's a good one. I'm a wheel-wright by profession. I learned the trade back east from a man who built Conestogas. I planned to go into business at Fort Pitt, but Bewilderness will do just as well. I can teach you my trade, Ben. That way we can both make some extra money. In fact, I've been thinkin' maybe we can start the business right off, soon as we arrive. Afore we even start on the cabin. Make some money right away." That should give Ben's confidence a boost, Aaron thought.

"A trade! You'd teach me?"

"Sure will, son." Aaron nodded, relieved and thrilled that Ben liked the idea. He wanted to do something in return for all his help. "I always planned on having a son and teaching it to him, but that never happened."

"I'd be proud to learn the trade from you, Mr. Fletcher. Fact is, I've been hankerin' to learn one but couldn't afford to go east for the training." He flushed with pleasure at the thought. Ben Allyn, businessman! His mother would have been proud of him.

Aaron smiled to himself. *What a nice young man.*

Money right away, Ben thought. *That's what I need. Nothing like earning money to make a man feel like a man!* Ben suddenly recalled something he had heard at the settlement.

"There's supposed to be more wagons coming through. I heard some talk about it. They'll probably need repair after crossing the mountains. I've seen some of those wagon wheels, all busted up from jolting over rocks and boulders. Stretches of that wagon road aren't road at all, they're dry creek beds. We should have lots of business and no competition. At Fort Pitt, they probably already have a wheelwright."

Aaron suppressed a smile. He liked ambition in people. Ben saw the opportunity and was prepared to take it on. He would make a good partner. He was honest, hard-working, and intelligent. Hopefully, he would be his son-in-law as well. Ben's pining looks at Molly had not gone unnoticed.

Molly, herself, was far from immune to the rugged young man's clean-cut good looks. She had given him enough encouragement too. Like that stunt she pulled sneaking out of the wagon to get her shoes with just her nightgown and a blanket on. And flashing her bare ankles at him! If her mother had seen her, what would she have said? He shuddered to think!

He had realized she was up to something and that it had to do with Ben, but he didn't expect her to do something so shocking. She had been pretty noisy climbing out of that wagon too! And she took her sweet old time getting back with her shoes. He was surprised she didn't knock a pot over just to make sure Ben noticed. That girl! Aaron managed to hide his humor.

Ben had been mulling over what Aaron had said and asked hesitatingly, "A man can make money at the trade, can't he? Enough to"—he paused—"support a family?"

Aaron kept his face serious. He had wondered before what was holding the boy back from speaking to Molly—now he understood. Of course, he should have known. Ben Allyn was a responsible young man. He knew what it was to be in want and would never ask a girl to share his life with him unless he could provide for her.

"If a man's willing to work hard, he can make a handsome living," Aaron assured him. He saw Ben relax and even smile a little. It seemed to Aaron the smile was tinged with relief.

"Why don't you go on up ahead," Aaron suggested, wanting to leave the two alone together. "Let me stay here by myself and gather my thoughts together. All of 'em." He leaned back on the warm wooden seat contentedly.

Ben was glad to leave Aaron to his thoughts. He had thoughts of his own and they were all bound up in a blond-haired girl. Ben felt infinitely better. For the first time, he didn't feel like a burden to the Fletchers. He was needed. He believed he was even wanted. Moreover, he had prospects. He would have a trade, a farm, and a cabin. Would he have a girl as well? The anxiety gnawed at him. He surely hoped so. A girl like Molly could have her choice of men. Was it presumptuous of him to think she would look favorably upon him?

Just then, Molly chose that moment to turn back and look at him. She smiled. It was a beautiful smile and, most important, it was an encouraging smile. Ben was entranced. Two dimples creased her pink cheeks. It was enough for Ben. His storm cloud evaporated instantly.

Ben glanced over at Aaron who apparently didn't notice him, so engrossed was he in the road, the trees, the sky, the passing landscape, the birds—everything but the two young people. Realizing he had no audience, Ben jogged ahead easily till he overtook and passed the slow-moving wagon then came up to where Molly was walking, swinging her bonnet by its strings.

"We're almost there." She smiled at him happily.

"Yes." Ben nodded, suddenly at a loss for words. As they walked together, Ben sidled a little closer until their arms almost touched. Then his hand crept over and sought hers. Although she breathed a little more quickly, she allowed his fingers to interlace with hers. They looked at each other and smiled, then blushed.

"I've been talking with your father," Ben started awkwardly.

"Yes," she encouraged him breathlessly.

"We've decided to start his business in Bewilderness right away. I'm going to be his partner and he's going to teach me his trade."

"That will be wonderful, Ben!" She was pleased her father thought so highly of him. Her eyes were like stars.

"That means we won't be able to start building the cabin until we get the business up and running. It means living in the wagon for a while longer. Is that all right with you?"

"Oh, yes. Whatever you think is best." She looked up at him through her dark lashes. As Molly had hoped, Ben couldn't resist. Taking her by the elbow, he rushed her ahead past a bend in the road out of sight of the rumbling, snail-paced wagon. When they were out of Aaron's sight, Ben leaned down and kissed her on the cheek.

When he pulled away, she whispered, "Oh, dear." Then she put a hand to her cheek and touched where he had kissed it.

"Do you mind?"

"No, I don't mind at all!" And to prove this, she reached up and kissed his lean brown cheek. It emboldened him to say what he wanted to say all along.

"When we build that cabin, Molly, should we make

two bedrooms or three? If we got married, we would only need two." He watched her stunned expression. He wanted to make his intentions perfectly clear.

"I think two would be fine," she responded at last. Molly's face reddened with embarrassment and pleasure. Ben relaxed and smiled.

"Will you marry me, Molly? When we get to Bewilderness?"

She sneaked a look at him, gratified and flattered to see how admiration and love glowed warmly in his gray eyes. "I'd like that very much."

"Good." He grinned at her. "Then it's a bargain. We ought to seal that bargain." He put his hands on her shoulders and kissed her lips. She returned his kiss as he slid his arms around her and held her close. They finally pulled apart when they heard the wagon rattle along the rutted track into view. Ben took Molly's hand in his as they continued walking ahead of the wagon. Aaron saw it and grinned. Thank goodness that was settled!

Chapter Twenty-one

As Rusty and Isabelle neared the fort the next day, they came upon some settlements. Rusty told the inhabitants about the massacre and they promised to raise a party of men to bury the dead. While he was there, he asked if there was a family around by the name of Trelawney. Nobody had heard of them. Rusty was puzzled.

He told Isabelle but assured her that they would ask at the fort. He didn't notice that Isabelle looked uneasy.

"Don't you worry, Little Bit. We'll find your folks. I brought you this far and I'll get you all the way home." Isabelle nodded vacantly.

Rusty saw this and was perplexed. He tried again. "You should be feeling pretty happy right about now. Your aunt and uncle will welcome you into their home.

223

Maybe they have children of their own you can play with. Wouldn't that be nice?"

Isabelle bit her lip and nodded.

"Don't be so worried. You'll see. Everything will turn out just fine."

Isabelle raised her anxious little face. "Promise, Rusty?" she asked urgently.

"Sure, I promise."

At the fort, everything was a-bustle. People were coming and going, taking trips, trading or just plain visiting. Rusty told Isabelle to wait with the horses while he spoke to the officer in charge.

Colonel Trent shook his head sadly over news of the massacre and promised to send some soldiers along with the settlers to take care of the dead. At the mention of the little girl, he frowned. "Trelawney? No, the name does not sound familiar. Let me ask my wife."

Her help was enlisted, but she was very sure that no settlers around there were named Trelawney. However, there was a family by the name of Pollard who had been waiting for their little niece from Boston. The girl's name was Ruby. Unfortunately, the family was killed last week when they went berrying.

Rusty was shocked. *Ruby? And no family?*

"But don't you worry about that little girl." She gave a tight smile that was meant to denote friendliness. "Lots of people will want her."

Rusty was relieved.

"Oh yes," she continued. "Mrs. Johnson needs a servant to help her and Mrs. Chadwick could use someone in the kitchen. She has six children and a seventh on the way. Another pair of hands would be a boon. If not, Mrs. Collingsworth does sewing and could train her."

"But," Rusty groped around for the words, "isn't there anyone who would want to adopt her as their daughter? She's a bright little thing, and cute."

Mrs. Trent laughed derisively and looked at her husband as if to say, "Men!"

"I'm afraid there is no one here, Mr. McBride. People have their own children. A farmer might want another child, but it would have to be a boy to help with the crops and hunting. A girl would be of no value to him."

Rusty felt her voice had all the warmth of ice. "Well, I wasn't expecting—"

"Of course you weren't," she soothed. "You just leave her to me. I'll see that she makes her way."

"But I took care of her for the last five days—"

"And I'm sure you did a wonderful job." She prodded him out the door. "But now it's a woman's task to find her a place. Don't worry, Mr. McBride"—she cut him off as he started to speak—"your duty is over."

He stood helplessly watching as Mrs. Trent went over to Isabelle, who was standing next to the horses. At the sight of the strange woman descending upon her, Isabelle looked alarmed and huddled closer to the animals.

"Now, young lady. Mr. McBride tells me you have been lying about your name. You have been calling yourself Isabelle Trelawney. But that isn't your name, is it? It's really Ruby Pollard, isn't that correct?" Isabelle looked at Rusty, who cravenly glanced away. "Well, is your name Ruby?"

Isabelle's eyes filled with tears. She hung her head. "Yes."

"Ha! I thought so." She looked at Rusty as if to indicate how easy it was for her, a woman, to get at the truth. "Why did you tell a horrible lie and say your name was Isabelle?"

Isabelle trembled. "Because I never liked the name Ruby."

"Never liked the name? A very frivolous reason, my girl. Do you know what happens to liars? They come to no good. Now, your aunt and uncle died last week and you haven't a soul in the world to take care of you." For a moment she looked as if this was Isabelle's fault. Isabelle looked guilty. "If you are willing to work and stop lying, I think I can find you a place to stay. You will have to work hard, though, to earn your keep. Are you willing to do that?"

"Yes, ma'am," she said in a small voice.

"Come along then. Mr. McBride has his business to attend to. You should be glad he saved your life and took care of you all this time. He can't be expected to be burdened with you forever. Now say 'Thank you.' "

Isabelle looked up at Rusty, blinking back tears. "Thank you, Mr. McBride." Her quavering voice was barely audible. Her face fell, and her thin little shoulders drooped under the frayed cotton dress. She suddenly realized Rusty was going away without her.

"Wait a minute." Rusty walked over to his pack and rummaged around till he found what he wanted. Then he walked back and kneeled in front of Isabelle.

"Here, Little Bit." He put a doll into her small hands. It was the doll he had picked up at the massacre. "Don't forget me." He put his arms around her and hugged her for several moments. She stood there stiff as a board looking as if her little heart was broken. Then Rusty stood up.

"Good-bye, Isabelle." He put his hand on her shoulder and felt it quiver. He bent down and kissed her cheek. It was damp. She kept her eyes on his shirt front and wouldn't look into his face.

"I'll be stopping by in a few months to see how you're doing," he said, trying to be cheerful.

"Mr. McBride! Her name is Ruby! Please don't encourage her! And when you call by again, you will find Ruby hard at work. As she should be." She nodded curtly at Rusty and dragged the little girl off. Her spirit broken, she followed Mrs. Trent still clutching her doll and doeskin bag.

"Hell and damnation!" He watched as the little woebegone figure was taken to a storefront. *Damn it, you cannot take in a little girl. What the hell do you know about them? She'll be much better off with women around as an example.* He offered the sop to his conscience. When he thought about Mrs. Trent, he winced.

She didn't seem to appreciate Little Bit—how smart she was, how loyal, how grateful.

He went into Ford's to trade and told him he'd pick up his goods later.

"Where's your little girl?" Ford asked curiously.

"She wasn't mine. I picked her up at the massacre. Mrs. Trent is going to find a family to take her in." He was curt.

"I see." Ford's eyes were speculative. "Too bad. She was a nice little thing. Seems like good company."

"I don't need company," Rusty said forcibly.

"Maybe she does," Ford said mildly. Feeling his censure, Rusty left, heading for the stables. He saw Isabelle sweeping out a storefront, slowly, unhappily. Already they were getting free labor out of her! That's it! He'd had enough! Cursing loudly, he stomped back into the store.

"I need some candy and some lengths of calico," he told Mrs. Ford.

"About four yards each?" she inquired innocently. "That would be enough for a dress and bonnet."

He looked at her, almost annoyed. "Yes," he finally mumbled, "and give me some red. She likes red." Smiling broadly, Mrs. Ford measured it off and wrapped it up.

"Bless you, Mr. McBride," she said, gently touching his sleeve. He turned beet red and left hurriedly. Stuffing the packages into one of his packs, he took the reins and started leading his horses to where Isabelle was sitting. He stopped directly in front of her. She had to look up.

"I'm looking for a partner to help me at my trading post. Know of anyone who could do it?" he asked. Isabelle looked up and stared at him for what seemed like minutes. Then he saw the spark of hope dawning in her eyes.

"I–I could," she began in a low voice, not really sure if he meant it. "I could be real helpful."

"Well then, you've got yourself a job. Come on, up you go." Isabelle watched him as if she couldn't believe it, then she jumped up and ran the few steps to him. He caught her and held her briefly as she hugged him hard. He could feel the hot tears squeezing through her tightly closed lids.

"No crying," he said gruffly as he swung her onto the horse behind him. She put her arms around his waist and clung to him. Her face was pressed against his back as if she was afraid to let go.

Mr. and Mrs. Ford smiled broadly as they watched the dark, good-looking trader leave with the tiny blond girl.

"It'll do him good," Mrs. Ford predicted.

As for Mrs. Trent, she was horrified to see an extra pair of free hands slipping away from her.

"Mr. McBride! Come back!" She waved her handkerchief at him agitatedly.

"Good-bye, Mrs. Trent!" Rusty took off his hat to her and clapped it back on.

"Well, partner, let's go pick up Bessie. She's probably wondering what happened to us by now."

Chapter Twenty-two

Joe Wilder was on his porch smoking contentedly when the trio came into Bewilderness. He enjoyed the afternoon before the surveyors came back from work. It was nice to sit quietly on a sunny day with only his dog for company. He took his pipe out of his mouth. "Mother! Come take a look!" Mrs. Wilder hurried out to see what was the matter. Joe pointed his pipe stem towards the trundling wagon. "Ain't that the Fletcher wagon?"

"It sure is. And look! Isn't that Ben Allyn walking there in front? I knew it! I just knew he didn't leave town with that Brisco fella and that pair of thieves. People said so, but I told you he would never be in their company. A nice, hard-working young man like that wouldn't want anything to do with them!" Her voice was contemptuous.

"'Lo folks!" Joe called out, waving to them as he rose from his seat. Joe noticed that Molly and Ben Allyn were holding hands. With her sharp eyes, Mrs. Wilder noticed it too.

"Hello," Aaron said, smiling tiredly as Ben gave him a hand to help him off the wagon. Molly was pleased to see he needed only a hand.

"You left the wagon train?" Mrs. Wilder asked, her eyes bright with curiosity.

"Not exactly," Aaron admitted. "We had to leave the train. I took sick real bad and the Millers decided we were too much of a burden. But we met up with Ben, and he escorted us back here, driving the wagon."

Mrs. Wilder's eyes were speculative, but she said nothing. Ben had assisted the Fletchers and that was that! No one's business why he had come to be out there in the woods in the first place. Perhaps he'd seen Molly from afar and been moonstruck—so he followed the wagon. She liked to think so. Mrs. Wilder was a romantic soul.

"What a shame," she said sympathetically. "Those Millers. I took a dislike to them right off and I don't often do that, do I, Joe?"

"Never does," he affirmed.

"But it's a blessing Ben came along. How are you feeling now, Mr. Fletcher?"

"Better, ma'am, better. It won't be long before I'll be as good as new. Just need a little more rest and staying put in one place." Then he told the Wilders how the wagon train had been massacred. They were aghast.

"Terrible! Too bad the Millers didn't know what they were doing!" Mrs. Wilder said. "It's a dangerous life out here. What will you do now? Wait for the next train going that way, I expect?"

"No." Aaron shook his head. "We've decided to take some land on Saylor Creek. Molly took a real fancy to it, and Ben and I are going to open a wheelwright business in town here."

Mrs. Wilder was vastly pleased. She always liked more neighbors, especially agreeable ones.

"Well, well. That's grand! For sure you've picked yourself a nice piece of property. Lots of people have eyed it up these past two years but they all went to Fort Pitt instead. Glad someone's got some sense to build on it. It'll make a fine farm."

"There's an empty building at the end of town." Joe took the pipe out of his mouth and pointed. "You could set up your business there. Fella who built it died about a year back. It's a strong building with plenty of room. No one would mind if ya just moved in."

Aaron looked pleased. "That's mighty kind of you. I reckon that's what we'll do then. Ben?"

Ben smiled, but he and Molly had been whispering quietly with their heads together. Now he spoke up. "Mrs. Wilder, do you know if there's any justice of the peace around? Molly and I"—he turned red—"would like to get married. That is"—Ben turned to Aaron—"if it's all right with you, sir."

Aaron was grinning. "Son, I couldn't think of a better man for my Molly!" He said it with such sincerity, Ben felt relieved. He supposed he should have asked his permission first, but he'd forgotten. Molly had a way of making him forget things.

"Tell ya what, boy," Joe added enthusiastically. "A preacher just come to town this morning. Goin' here and there, speakin' the good word and marryin' and baptizin' people. He's upstairs now." He turned to his smiling wife. "Mother, roust him up! Tell him he's got a weddin' to perform!"

As Mrs. Wilder hurried away, Ben turned to Molly who was beaming happily. They had a lifetime ahead of them and, right now, this half-civilized settlement smack dab in the middle of Indian country was a mighty fine place to start.

Ben pulled Molly into his arms and kissed her right in front of everybody. Their fresh faces aglow, Ben suddenly lifted her into the air and twirled her around. When he set her down, the good citizens of Bewilderness were gathering around, laughing and congratulating them wholeheartedly. They saw in these two young people the same hopes and plans that had brought them here as well. They wanted to see them succeed in this new land.

"We're going to build that cabin right away!" Ben declared so fervently that Molly, standing in the circle of his arm, blushed rosily. "Then we'll have a home—a real home!"

It had been a long time since Ben had a home, not

since his mother died when he was a boy, leaving him only a Bible and twelve dollars—all she had. Since then, there had been a series of cheap lodgings or sleeping in lean-tos. The world was a desolate place when no one cared if you came or went. He was just another lonely man roaming the frontier with great longings in his heart. Now he had finally found what he had been searching for: a home and family. It might not be much of a dream for some, but it was all Ben desired.

In his mind Ben could see that place on Saylor Creek. Its black, fertile soil would make a farm where a wilderness had been. He could see a home there, where a fire burned cheerfully and the smell of fresh-brewed coffee filled the air with its fragrance. And at the end of the day when the work was done, there would be a girl waiting for him.

Gone was the grave, sad young man. Smiling love had taken its place.

"We'll build that cabin with plenty of room," he announced, kissing Molly gently, reverently on the temple. "Because I intend to have a big family. Our house is going to be a-bustle with kids and relations."

He never wanted to be alone again.